LILY'S STORY, BOOK FOUR

IMPERFECT

This is a work of fiction. Any resemblance it bears to reality is entirely coincidental.

Life Imperfect (Lily's Story, Book 4)
Copyright © 2015 Christine Kersey
All rights reserved

LILY'S STORY, BOOK FOUR

# Life
## IMPERFECT

# CHRISTINE KERSEY

SAPPHIRE
CREEK
PRESS

# Books by Christine Kersey

### Lily's Story Series
*He Loves Me Not (Lily's Story, Book 1)*
*Don't Look Back (Lily's Story, Book 2)*
*Love At Last (Lily's Story, Book 3)*
*Life Imperfect (Lily's Story, Book 4)*

### Parallel Trilogy
*Gone (Parallel Trilogy, Book 1)*
*Imprisoned (Parallel Trilogy, Book 2)*
*Hunted (Parallel Trilogy, Book 3)*
*After (a parallel story)*
*The Other Morgan (a parallel story)*

### Over You — 2 book series
*Over You*
*Second Chances (sequel to Over You)*
*Melanie and Avery's Story — coming 2015*

### Standalone Books
*Suspicions*
*No Way Out*

# Acknowledgements

I want to thank my loyal beta readers for their willingness to read *Life Imperfect* and give me their feedback! I truly appreciate them and the time they spent helping me out. Their names are listed below, alphabetically by first name.

Abigail W.

Ali Fruit

Angela Macias Dial

Corinn Kendall

Ioana Clayton

Jennifer Dhillon

Kris Bird

Robyn Maitland

Shantel Anderson

Tiffini LeJeune

And a special thank you to my editor, Annette Fruit. You are the best!!

# Chapter One

When the doorbell rang, two-year-old Natalie looked up from the doll she was playing with, her vivid blue eyes questioning. I loved her eyes. They looked just like Trevor's, my deceased first husband. That was one feature that had drawn me to him right away, and though our marriage had ended violently, it was only due to that union that I had my daughter.

"Who could that be?" I asked with a smile.

She tossed her doll aside and scurried to the front door, then waited for me to open it.

Just as eager as Natalie, I hurried to the door and pulled it open. "Alyssa," I said with a smile, then pulled her into a hug. "It's so good to see you."

"You too," she said as she wrapped her arms around my shoulders.

"It's been too long."

I released her and invited her in.

She stepped into the entry, then knelt in front of Natalie. "Hello, beautiful girl. Do you remember me?"

"Of course she does," I said, my voice joyful. "We've been looking at pictures from your last visit." I ran my fingers through Natalie's soft baby hair. "Do you remember Aunt Alyssa?"

Natalie looked at Alyssa shyly, then nodded.

"She is so adorable," Alyssa said as she stood.

"Thanks."

"Is Jackson asleep?"

"Yes, but he's due to wake up any minute."

"Good. I can't wait to hold him."

"I was just about to have a late lunch," I said as I walked towards the kitchen. "Are you hungry after that long drive?"

"Actually, I kind of am."

I pulled out some lunch meat and bread and began making sandwiches. "How was the drive from Vegas?"

She leaned against the counter. "I left pretty early this morning, but the drive wasn't too bad."

"That's good." I glanced at her. "I need to get out there and see Trevor's parents. They haven't seen Jackson since he was born, and he's five months old."

Alyssa was quiet for a few moments. "I really admire how you've kept Trevor's parents in your life, Lily. I don't know if I could have done that. You know, after everything that happened with Trevor."

Glancing at her again, I said, "I want Natalie to know her grandparents. Especially since mine are no longer around." I smiled. "The more people who love her, the better."

"Yeah. That totally makes sense."

I carried the plates to the table and set them on the placemats, then turned to Alyssa. "How's Ty?"

She smiled, but it seemed to falter. "He's good."

I wondered what she wasn't telling me about her husband, but knew if she wanted to share whatever was troubling her, she'd tell me in time. I gestured for her to sit, then made sure Natalie was content with her doll before I sat as well. "What about your job? How's that going?"

"It's been busy. Las Vegas is a good place for those of us in the hospitality field. I'm glad I moved there."

"I'll bet. I'm just glad you were able to take a few days off for a visit."

She picked up her sandwich. "Me too. But I'll have to head back on Friday."

"Well, that gives us a couple of days to visit." At that moment I heard the unmistakable sound of Jackson waking up from his nap. Letting him fuss for a few minutes, I managed to eat half of my sandwich before pushing back from the table. "Motherhood calls," I said.

Alyssa laughed as I headed towards the hallway.

Pausing outside Jackson's door, I listened to his baby sounds before pushing the door open and walking to his crib. "Hi there, baby," I cooed. "We have a visitor today."

Jackson kicked his feet and smiled as I reached down and lifted him from the crib. I changed him, then carried him into the kitchen.

Alyssa held out her hands. "Oh my goodness. He is so cute. He's looking more and more like Marcus."

I set him in her arms. "Yes, he is definitely a mini-Marcus."

After only a moment, Jackson's chin quivered, then he began to wail. Alyssa looked stricken as she held him out to me.

I laughed. "He's just hungry." I walked to the couch and sat on the soft cushions. "You don't mind if I nurse him, do you?"

"Of course not."

I got Jackson settled and a few moments later Alyssa joined me on the couch in the family room.

"You're such a good mother, Lily."

Warmed by her kind words, I smiled. "Just as you will be one day."

She gazed at me, then her eyes filled with tears.

Horrified that I may have said something that had upset her, my face paled. "What's wrong?"

"Oh, Lily," she said as she took a tissue out of her purse and dabbed at her eyes. "Everything's wrong."

"What is it? What's going on?"

She shook her head as she stared at her lap, then she finally met my gaze. "It's Ty."

Imagining all sorts of awful things, I waited for her to go on.

"Do you remember on our Alaskan wedding cruise, how he spent so much time in the casino?"

My mind went back to the good feelings and fun time I'd had on their wedding cruise. Between Natalie's needs, and my budding friendship with Ty's best friend/best man Cameron, I hadn't paid a lot of attention to what Ty had been doing. "I guess so."

"Well, I hadn't realized it at the time, but—" A flush crept up Alyssa's cheeks. "Ty has a gambling problem. A serious one."

"Oh no." I gazed at Alyssa's worried face as I grasped for some words of comfort or wisdom. Nothing came to mind.

"I don't know what to do," she said. "I've talked to him about it, but he doesn't think there's anything wrong with spending hours at the casinos."

I didn't want to get too personal, but I also wanted to decide for myself if Alyssa was blowing this out of proportion. When we'd been going to school together at the University of Nevada, Reno, she'd second-guessed my decisions quite a bit. It had turned out she'd been right about Trevor, but still, I knew she could sometimes jump to conclusions.

"How much time are we talking about?" I asked.

"Sometimes he goes straight to the casinos after he gets off work."

She averted her gaze. "I do work a lot of evenings though."

"This isn't your fault."

She looked at me, her forehead wrinkled. "But he's told me he hates coming home to an empty house. Especially when he knows I won't be home for hours." Her chin dipped towards her chest. "He said that's why he goes to the casino."

That didn't sound like a gambling problem to me. More like a loneliness problem. "Alyssa."

She looked up and met my gaze.

"Can you change your hours? You know, so that you're gone less in the evenings?"

Her lips pressed into a straight line. "I tried that. But even when I'm home, he often goes to the casino. And then I end up sitting home alone."

Now *that* sounded like more of an issue.

"Lily?" Alyssa said, her voice beginning to shake.

"What?"

"Last night Ty and I had a huge fight. He told me he lost big yesterday, and now he owes the casino a lot of money. *A lot.*" Her eyebrows pulled together and she inhaled sharply through her nose before softly exhaling through her mouth, then she stared at me. "I left him, Lily." Her shoulders seemed to collapse inward as her body began to tremble. "I left him."

I lay Jackson across my lap, quickly adjusted my shirt, then moved to Alyssa's side. I placed my arm around her shoulders and tugged her against me as she cried. I wanted to say something to comfort her, but I'd been through enough of my own challenges to know that false words of hope did nothing to help. The best thing I could do was just be there for her and to make sure she knew that she could count on me. Always.

# Chapter Two

Once Alyssa gained control of her emotions, she filled in the details. "I told him I couldn't take it anymore and that if he refused to get help, I would leave." Her lips compressed. "He said there was nothing to get help with, and that he loved me, but that *I* was the one with a problem. That I had unrealistic expectations." With tears in her eyes, Alyssa asked, "Is that true? Am I being unrealistic in expecting my husband to spend time with me instead of at the casinos?"

"No," I said as I shook my head. "You're not being unrealistic. You have every right to expect him to want to be with you. You've been married less than two years, Alyssa."

"I know that. I do. That's why I told him I was leaving. Not just for this visit to you, but until he admits he needs help and then gets it."

I admired her strength. I knew it couldn't have been easy. When I'd

7

left Trevor after he'd become abusive, it had been the hardest thing I'd ever had to do in my life. Especially when I'd known I was pregnant with his child. But at least Ty wouldn't come after Alyssa and try to take her child, or try to kill her.

Memories of Trevor taking Natalie when she was a newborn, and then his attempt to strangle me to death sent tremors of remembered terror through me.

*He's gone now. Forever. And you have Marcus, who is the complete opposite of Trevor. He's loving, patient, kind. And now he's Natalie's legal father.*

A soft smile lifted the corners of my mouth as I thought about my husband and the wonderful life we'd built together. The months leading up to both of us admitting the way we felt had been rough, but it had been worth it.

"Don't lose hope," I said to Alyssa. "It might take time, but he's bound to realize what he's doing to you, and to himself."

"It's so hard," she said with tears in her voice. "So hard to sit by and watch him self-destruct."

"No one knows better than me how difficult it is to watch your spouse turn into someone you don't recognize," I said. "And the end result doesn't always turn out the way you want. But in the end, *you* will be stronger. And with hard work on both your parts, your marriage will be stronger too."

She smiled. "Thanks, Lily."

After that, Alyssa seemed to become calmer, and we talked about her issues with Ty, as well as other things, until Marcus got home from work that evening.

As I watched him greet Alyssa and chat with her for a few minutes, my heart bloomed with love for this man who had been there for me right when I needed him the most. I'd met him soon after moving to the California Central Valley, and though for my own safety I'd had to lie to him about my real name and my marriage to Trevor, he'd stood by me and I'd fallen in love with him.

"How's my little bruiser?" he said as he lifted Jackson from my arms.

"He's been good as gold, like usual," I said with a smile.

Marcus blew raspberries into Jackson's neck, making him giggle.

"Me, Daddy," Natalie said as she stood patiently waiting for her turn to have his attention.

A few minutes later Marcus took the children out back to play with them, giving Alyssa and me time to be alone.

"You are so lucky, Lily." A sad smile curved her mouth.

*I am lucky. Luckier than I ever thought I'd be.* "Ty loves you," I said. "Maybe right now he just needs some space to understand that what he's doing is hurting you and your marriage."

"I hope you're right."

That night after Alyssa had gone to bed in the guest room, Marcus and I finally had a moment alone. He pulled me into his arms and held me close and I reveled in the strength and security of his arms. I remembered how I'd almost turned him away when he'd wanted to marry me due to the ridiculous notion that I wasn't good enough for him. His mother's opinion had shaped that point of view, and it had taken Marcus's suggestion that we get married *that day*, as well as the encouragement of Trevor's mother Marcy, of all people, to convince me to marry him. I'd never regretted that decision. Not once.

"Are you having a good visit with Alyssa?" he asked as he sat on the bed and pulled me onto his lap.

"Yes, although she told me that she and Ty are having some challenges."

His eyebrows rose. "Oh yeah? What's going on?"

I told him what Alyssa had shared with me. "I feel so bad for her. I don't know how to help her."

"She probably just needs a friend," he said. "Someone to listen."

I nodded. "That's true."

He gazed at me a moment, then his eyebrows bunched. "I have

something I have to tell you."

The tone of his voice caught my attention, and alarm rippled through me. "What is it?"

"We had a company-wide meeting today. And, well . . ." His jaw tightened. "They've declared bankruptcy."

I went rigid on his lap. "What?"

He sighed. "Evidently the company had been having financial difficulties, so they brought in investors. The investors gave the company a deadline to fix some issues . . . and, well, the issues weren't fixed, so the investors are shutting the business down."

"Can they do that? They're just investors."

He grimaced. "The investors had a majority share. They can do whatever they want."

"But your job . . ."

"It no longer exists."

The alarm that had been nibbling at the edges of my consciousness rang louder, but I silenced it as I tried to think things through. "I used a lot of the money from my dad's life insurance policy when I bought the house, but I still have some of it left. Plus we have some money in savings. I suppose we can use that to pay the bills until you get another job." *But what if it takes him a long time to find a good job and the money runs out? Then what?* Panic threaded its way through me and my heart began to pound.

Gently, he stroked my face. "Don't worry, Lily. We'll figure it out. I have contacts. I'll find another job."

At his touch, my panic receded. He would make everything okay. I had complete trust in him. I sank against him as my racing heart slowed to its normal rhythm.

# Chapter Three

The next day Marcus got up at his usual time and prepared to leave as if he was going to work.

"What are your plans today?" I asked as I lay in our bed watching him. "Where are you going to go?"

"Rick and Jason are going to meet me at the coffee shop."

I pictured the two men who he worked with, and who were also now unemployed. "What are you guys going to do?"

"We're going to strategize, see what we can come up with. Then I might head over to the library with my laptop and use their wi-fi to job hunt." He kissed me lightly on the lips. "You can text me if you need anything."

"Okay." I smiled up at him, the feeling of security that his presence always gave me wrapping around me like a warm blanket.

Shortly after he left, Natalie and Jackson both woke up, and just as I finished feeding them, Alyssa walked into the family room.

"Good morning," I said, wondering if I should tell her about Marcus losing his job. She had enough worries of her own, and I wasn't sure I wanted to layer mine on top of them. "How did you sleep?"

"Okay. My mind kept going to Ty and whether or not he was at the casino. I almost texted him, but decided I should give him time to contact me first."

I nodded. "Probably a good idea." Although secretly I wondered how long it would take him to feel Alyssa's absence. If he was truly addicted to gambling, it might take a while.

"Marcus looks good," she said. "And I can tell you're both so happy."

I pushed a smile onto my mouth, knowing if she'd said that the day before I would have agreed with enthusiasm. Now, with Marcus's job situation unclear, my usual joy was tempered with worry. "We are," I said, not quite ready to share my bad news.

*Maybe Marcus will come up with a solution and there won't be a need to tell anyone about my concerns.*

Ready to change the subject, I said, "Do you have anything you want to do today?"

"Maybe check out that cute boutique you told me about."

"Sounds great."

A moment later, Greta, my treasured German Shepherd, came through her doggie door. Natalie ran to her and threw her arms around her. Greta's tail swung in a wide arc.

We spent the rest of the day running errands and visiting, and though I enjoyed spending time with Alyssa, in the back of my mind I kept thinking about Marcus and wondering how his job hunt was going. How long would it take him to find another job? Would his pay be as much as we were used to?

"What's wrong, Lily?" Alyssa asked after I'd put the children down for naps and we'd settled on the couch for a quiet chat.

"What do you mean?"

"I know you. Something's on your mind."

I sighed, and decided to tell her my news. At a minimum it would take her mind off of her problems. "Last night Marcus told me his company shut down." I frowned. "He lost his job."

Alyssa sat up straighter. "Oh no." Then she looked thoughtful. "He's an electrical engineer, right?"

"Yes, but he didn't graduate very long ago and he doesn't have very much experience."

"Still, he's smart. I'll bet he finds another job really fast."

"I hope so."

When Marcus got home that afternoon, I was anxious to hear how his day had gone, but I wanted to discuss it with him in private. He chatted with Alyssa and me for a few minutes, then headed to our bedroom.

"I'll be back in a bit," I said to Alyssa.

She smiled knowingly. "No rush. I'll keep an eye on Natalie."

"Thanks." With Jackson in my arms, I headed to the bedroom where I found Marcus sitting on the foot of our bed doing something on his phone. "How'd your day go?"

He looked up. "Hey, sweetie." Then he held out his arms for Jackson, who I handed over. Marcus nuzzled his neck. "He always smells so fresh. I don't know how you keep him smelling so good."

I laughed as I sat beside him. "He gets it from you." I kissed his neck. "You always smell good too."

With his free arm, he drew me against him. "What did I ever do to deserve you?"

I lay my head against his shoulder. "Are you trying to avoid answering my question?"

He laughed. "I can't get anything by you."

I pulled away and looked at him. "No, you can't."

A wide smile filled his face. "All right. You got me."

I smiled in return. "Tell me about your day."

"Like I told you this morning, I met with Rick and Jason." A nervous smile lifted the corners of his mouth. "Well, after a lot of talking, we came up with the idea to start our own firm."

"What do you mean?" I asked. "Doing what exactly?"

"The same thing we've been doing at our old firm."

"How much will that cost? How will you pay for it?" The idea that we would have to pay for a new business on top of needing to pay the bills seriously stressed me out.

Marcus chuckled softly. "That's what I need to talk to you about."

A bad feeling grew within me. "What do you mean?"

"I think you can tell where this is going," Marcus said. "Between the three of us who want to start this business, I'm the only one who actually has the cash."

"You mean *I'm* the only one who has the cash." I didn't mean to sound snarky, but the memory of Trevor locking me up and stealing my money flashed into my mind, and I couldn't help my defensive attitude.

Marcus sighed. "Look, Lily, I completely understand if you don't want to loan me any of your money, but if I want to be part of this, I have to bring cash to the table." Reticence crossed his face. "I suppose I can always apply for a small business loan."

"That would mean more debt for us."

"Yes, it would. But what else can I do?"

"So would Rick and Jason bring money to the table too?"

"Yes. We'd all bring in an equal share."

"And it would just be a loan?"

"Yes," Marcus said, then he paused. "But I don't know how long it would take before I could pay you back."

The thought of not having my nest egg to fall back on made my stomach churn—even if I knew he would eventually pay me back. "I just don't know."

"Take some time to think about it," he said. "The three of us are meeting again tomorrow to see where we stand. I can tell them I'm still working on my share."

"How soon would you need the money?"

"Our old firm is selling off their equipment for a bargain price, so if we want to take advantage of it, we need to jump on it."

"Okay." I paused. "Have you thought about how you're going to do things differently than your old firm? You know, so you don't make the same mistakes they did?"

"Of course. We're not going in to this blind, Lily. Jason has a lot of experience on the business side of things." He smiled. "We're going to do things as cheaply as possible."

That reassured me, but I was still wary. "What if you can't pay me back?"

Marcus pulled away and stared at me. "What are you suggesting? That we'll fail?" His eyes shone with hurt. "You don't have much faith in me, do you?"

"It's not that," I began. "It's just . . ." I sighed softly. "Besides the little we have in savings, it's all we have for emergencies."

"I'm well aware of that." A tone of irritation clouded his voice. "Don't you think I know that?" He sighed. "I don't need you to remind me that we didn't have a lot of extra money before I lost my job."

Guilt and frustration swept over me. "I'm not blaming you. I appreciate all you do for us." I reached up and gently stroked his face. "If it wasn't for you, I can't imagine where I'd be. I love being home with our children, and I couldn't do that without your support—emotional as well as financial." I held his gaze. "Marcus, I love you." I waited a beat, wanting him to know my next question wasn't tied to my love for him. "I have to ask though. Have the three of you figured out how you're going to find clients? I mean, how long will it take before you're actually making any money?"

"All three of us have worked with clients that are now without an engineering firm. I'm sure some of them will sign with us."

"How much experience do the other two men have?"

Marcus sighed, clearly feeling exasperated by all of my questions. "Between the three of us, we have at least twenty years experience."

"That's good," I said, almost to myself. "But how long until you turn a profit?"

"I don't know, but it'll probably be a while." He stood and began pacing. "Can I just say that I don't like having my wife question me like she's my banker?" He stopped and faced me, his forehead furrowed. "Any other questions?"

I didn't like his vague answer on when they'd be making money, although I knew there was no way he could know for sure. "Do you need *all* of my nest egg? I mean, maybe we should keep some back to pay bills."

His jaw tightened. "You know, just forget it, Lily. I think it would be better if I just applied for a small business loan."

I jumped up and went to him, placing my hands on his shoulders. "Marcus, please don't be angry with me. I just have to . . . well, I'm just nervous about this."

With a soft voice, he said, "It would help if you had more faith in me."

"I do have faith in you. I do."

"But you just don't want to loan me the money." It came out as a statement.

He was right. I wanted everything to go back to how it was—Marcus going to work each day and bringing home a steady paycheck, and my inheritance tucked safely away in the bank, available for emergencies.

But wasn't this an emergency? Marcus needed what I had. Why couldn't I let it go? What was more important? The money in the bank, or my husband? Besides, did I want him to dig a deeper hole by putting us into debt with a small business loan?

As I gazed into his face, I thought about all the things he'd done for me and knew it was my turn to do something for him. Though still

16

filled with trepidation, I decided to take a leap of faith. "I'll loan you the money."

He stared at me like he was waiting for me to change my mind. And I wanted to, but I kept my lips firmly pressed together.

"Are you sure?" he finally asked.

The only thing I was sure of was that I loved him and that I had to show him that I had faith in him. It would be hard to hand over my money, but ultimately, he was more important. Besides, we would still have some money available in our savings with which to pay the bills. I nodded.

He leaned towards me and pressed his lips to mine. "Thank you. This means a lot to me."

The happiness on his face helped convince me I'd made the right decision. "You're welcome."

"Why don't you let me make dinner tonight," he said. "That way you and Alyssa can relax and talk."

He didn't make dinner often, and I couldn't help but feel like he was just doing it because he was happy that I'd agreed to loan him the money—but I wasn't going to call him on it. "Thanks, honey. I appreciate that."

# Chapter Four

As Alyssa and I talked and kept an eye on Natalie, I listened to Marcus working in the kitchen and wondered if I'd made the right decision.

*What if they can't get enough clients? What if the money I loaned him isn't enough and he needs more? I have money in a trust for Natalie, but surely he would never think to ask for that.*

Alyssa leaned towards me and whispered, "Does he cook dinner often?"

Forcing my thoughts away from the worst case scenarios, I smiled. "Actually, no. Not very often at all." I hadn't told her about my loan to Marcus—and I didn't plan to.

She glanced towards the kitchen. "I think it's awesome. Even if it's not very often." Her smile faltered. "Ty's hardly home, let alone in the kitchen making dinner for me."

Relieved to think about something besides my newfound concerns, I focused on Alyssa. "You just barely made the decision to leave him." I gazed at her steadily. "You've been gone for one day now. How are you feeling about your decision? Do you still think it's the right thing to do?"

Alyssa ran her hands over her face, then sighed as she looked at me. "I don't know." She stared at the blank wall for a moment. "At first it seemed like the only thing I could do to get his attention. But now I'm not so sure about it."

"You're allowed to change your mind, you know." I smiled softly.

"I know I am. But if I go back now, what message will that send to Ty?" Her lips pressed into a straight line. "Next time—if there is a next time—he won't believe me when I say I'm going to leave."

I didn't say anything, my thoughts scattered on Alyssa's problems, as well as my own.

"Even if I stay away," Alyssa began, "there's no guarantee Ty will change." She sighed. "I suppose I need to remember why I fell in love with him in the first place."

Nodding absently, I briefly thought about my own experience with a husband who did things I didn't like. There hadn't been anything I could have done to change who Trevor had been. Leaving had been my only option. "The only person you have control over is yourself," I said. "You can't count on your actions changing him. All you can do is control the way you respond to him."

A small smile lifted the corners of her mouth. "I know. But it's just so hard." She laughed quietly. "If I could just get him to do what I want, everything would be fine."

My eyebrows rose as I nodded. "If only."

"Dinner's ready," Marcus said.

I put Natalie in her high chair, then sat at the table with Marcus and Alyssa.

"This looks delicious," Alyssa said.

I nodded. "It sure does."

Marcus laughed. "You're just saying that because you didn't have to make it."

I smiled. "That may have something to do with it, but it really does look yummy."

"Thanks."

The sound of Jackson waking up filtered into the kitchen, and I glanced at Marcus. "He has impeccable timing."

"He just wants to eat too," he said as he pushed back from the table and headed towards the hallway. A few moments later he returned with Jackson held against his chest. "You ladies eat and I'll try to keep him entertained until you can nurse him."

"I'll hurry," I said.

"No, don't rush. He can wait a few minutes." Jackson fussed, but Marcus put a pacifier in his mouth, which settled him down.

As I watched him with our son, I knew I'd been beyond lucky to have found him. He was a good man, a good husband and father, and hardworking to boot. Glad now that I'd decided to loan him the money, the stress I'd been feeling seemed to melt away.

The next morning Alyssa told me Ty had called her after she'd gotten in bed the night before.

"What did he say?" I asked as I bounced Jackson in my arms.

"He asked when I was coming home."

"What did you say?"

She pursed her lips. "I asked him why I should come home when he's hardly ever there. He told me I was exaggerating." She frowned. "I told him I didn't know when I'd be coming home, and then we hung up."

"What are you going to do?"

"I have to go back to work tomorrow, so obviously I actually *will* have to go home to Vegas. But I know they'll let me stay in one of their rooms for a reduced rate for a while."

"Oh, Alyssa. I'm so sorry this is happening."

"I'm just so frustrated with him," she said, her voice strained. "It seems like he's changed so much since our wedding." Her frown deepened. "Or maybe he was like this all along and I just didn't want to see it." She looked thoughtful. "If you don't mind me asking, when did you realize that Trevor wasn't exactly who you thought he was?"

I hadn't thought a lot about Trevor and our relationship in a long time. He'd been dead for two years, and though his family was a part of my life, we rarely talked about him. And Marcus never wanted to talk about him—which was fine with me.

"You don't have to talk about it if it makes you uncomfortable," Alyssa said.

"No, that's okay," I said. "I just haven't thought about that in a while." I glanced at Natalie as she played with her doll on the floor. "When I look back on it, I can see the signs were there from the beginning. I just didn't want to see them. I wanted to believe what I wanted to believe." I smiled in remembrance. "You were there. You even tried to warn me. But I wouldn't listen."

Alyssa laughed. "Yeah, you were stubborn."

"No. I just thought I was in love." A smile blossomed on my mouth. "I didn't know what love really was. Not until I met Marcus."

"I'm glad you found each other," Alyssa said. "I can definitely see that he makes you happy."

She was right. He did make me happy. I hoped I made him happy too. I wondered how his meeting with his two friends was going. Had they been able to convince their wives to pony up their share? Or were they as nervous about it as I was?

"Maybe after a few more days of you being gone," I began, "Ty will realize that you're serious about wanting him to change."

Alyssa shook her head. "I hope so. I really want to make this marriage work."

"All marriages go through rough patches," I said, thinking that

Marcus and I had been able to avoid any of those so far. "But most people work things out because they love each other."

"I do love him. No question about that."

"Then you have the basics down." Jackson had fallen asleep against my shoulder. "I'll be right back," I whispered, then I carried him to his room and lay him in his crib. A moment later I returned to the family room. "Hopefully he'll sleep for a while."

"How's Marcus's job hunt going? Any luck yet?"

I hesitated for only a moment. "Actually, he's decided to start his own firm with two of his former co-workers."

Alyssa smiled. "That's exciting." Then after gazing at me for a moment, her eyebrows pulled together. "You don't look excited."

"I'm too easy to read, aren't I?"

"Sometimes." She laughed. "No, all the time."

I laughed with her, then my humor seeped away. "I liked how things were, but he really wants to do this."

"What's the worst that could happen?"

Several scenarios flashed through my mind. "I guess that we go broke, can't afford to pay our mortgage, and end up losing the house."

"That would be bad," she said. "But if everyone's healthy, then it wouldn't be the end of the world."

"That's another thing. We'd have to get health insurance, and that's so expensive." My anxiety went up a notch.

"You guys will figure it out."

I smiled, but her words didn't do anything to assuage my concerns.

---

After I cleaned up from dinner that evening, I asked Alyssa to keep an eye on Natalie so I could talk to Marcus. Jackson was in Marcus's arms as I followed him to our bedroom. I sat on the foot of the bed while Marcus stood in front of me, gently bouncing Jackson in his arms.

"Tell me about your meeting," I said.

"We all want to do this. It's just a matter of when everyone can pull the money together."

I nodded. "What kind of timing are you looking at?"

"Jason thinks he'll be able to get his share by sometime next week. Rick, though, might take a little more time." Marcus chuckled. "His wife isn't fully on board yet."

I kept my expression neutral, but inside I was glad to know I wasn't the only one who was hesitant about this new venture.

"Even though we're waiting on the rest of the funds," he said, "we're moving forward with our plans."

"What do you mean? What exactly are you doing?"

Marcus shifted from one foot to the other, like he was less than eager to tell me what they were going to do. "We've begun researching office space. We've also put in a bid to buy the equipment from my old firm."

Hearing him list the specific things they were going to do, and knowing those things were going to cost money, I felt a new tremor of worry pulse through me. "I see."

"Don't worry, Lily. Besides the equipment we're bidding for, we haven't committed to anything yet."

I tried to hide my relief, but Marcus knew me well enough to read my thoughts.

He turned away from me, but not before I saw his jaw tighten. "I think Jackson needs his diaper changed," he said, then he left the room.

I sighed softly as I shook my head, then I went back into the family room.

# Chapter Five

When it was time for Alyssa to leave the next morning, I drew her into my arms and told her to call me if she needed anything.

"It was wonderful to visit with you, Lily," she said after I released her. "I appreciate all your words of wisdom."

I laughed. "I don't know that I had many of those."

She smiled. "You did. Besides, it was nice just to have someone listen to my problems." Her smile changed to a frown. "I'm not ready to tell my family what's going on."

"I understand."

"Next time you're in Vegas, come see me."

"I will."

When Marcus came home that afternoon, I was glad to see him. I'd worked on getting over my apprehension about him moving forward with his business plans, and I determined that I would be more supportive, even if I still had several layers of worry.

"I'm glad you're home," I said as I wrapped my arms around his neck.

"Oh yeah? Why's that?"

"Because I always love it when you're home."

He pulled me close and I savored the strength and security of him. He'd never let me down and I knew I could trust him completely. After my experiences with Trevor, knowing I had a man by my side who I never had to doubt, never had to second guess, gave me a feeling of safety like I'd never known before.

"I love to come home to you, Lily," he murmured in my ear.

I wrapped my arms around his neck and snuggled close.

"Mommy," Natalie said as she tugged on my jeans. "Mommy, I hungry."

Reluctantly, I extricated myself from Marcus's embrace and turned to Natalie. But before I could tend to her needs, Marcus picked her up and said, "What do you want, sweet pea? Daddy'll get it for you."

My heart warmed as I watched the way he interacted with Natalie. He'd been in my life since before she'd been born. When I'd been in the hospital after Natalie's birth, and my supposedly deceased husband had shown up, Marcus had been understandably upset. It had taken some time for him to get over the hurt that I'd lied to him. But eventually he'd come to understand my reasons, and ever since, he'd been my fiercest ally.

*I'm the luckiest woman I know.*

---

The next day, Trish, Marcus's mother, invited the children and me over for lunch and I happily agreed. Though our relationship had started out rocky, once Marcus had let his mother know that he loved me and was going to marry me regardless of how she felt, she'd come around, and ever since then we'd had a good relationship.

Deep inside I'd harbored the hope that my mother-in-law would be like a mother to me, but that hadn't happened yet, and I wasn't so sure it ever would. But I did have Marcy—Trevor's mother and my first mother-in-law. Despite everything, we'd become good friends and she and her husband had been nothing but supportive.

"He's such a beautiful baby," Trish said as she took Jackson from my arms when we arrived for our luncheon. She glanced at me then gazed at my son. "He looks so much like Marcus did when he was that age."

"He's such an easy baby too," I said as Natalie and I followed her inside. "Was Marcus like that?"

Trish laughed as we sat in her living room. "No. He was a fussy baby. Drove me crazy for the first six months of his life."

I laughed with her. "Well, I'm glad Jackson is more like Natalie." I smiled at my two-year-old, who sat at my feet playing with her favorite doll.

Trish smiled at Natalie. "Yes, she's always been so good at entertaining herself." Trish looked at me. "You're very fortunate, Lily."

"I know I am." My mind went to Marcus. *In more ways than one.*

Trish's mind must have gone in the same direction, because she said, "Marcus sure is excited about this new business he's starting."

"Yes. Although to be honest, it's stressing me out." Even though I knew Trish would staunchly support anything Marcus did, it seemed safe to tell her how I really felt.

"Oh? Why's that? I know it can be scary to go out on your own with a business, but are you having doubts?"

The tone of her voice made me think she didn't approve of me expressing any doubts whatsoever. Not in her son. "Not exactly," I said, wondering if I should tell her what I was thinking.

She moved Jackson to her shoulder. "Then why are you feeling stressed?"

"Honestly, it's the financial part of things. Now that he's not drawing a paycheck, I'm worried about paying our bills."

"Well, it takes money to make money. You know that, right?"

"Of course. But it also takes money to pay the mortgage."

Trish smiled, but it seemed forced. "You need to give Marcus time. It's only been a few days and they're just getting started."

Obviously she didn't understand my concerns, so I let the matter drop. When I got home later that afternoon, I decided to call Marcy. As much as she liked Marcus, surely she wouldn't feel the need to defend him or take his side. But as it turned out, after she commiserated with me on my worries, she had concerns of her own.

"You have money in a trust for Natalie, right?" she asked.

I thought about the money I'd dug up in the desert—money it had turned out Trevor and Rob had won gambling. I'd taken Trevor's share and put it in a trust for Natalie. "Yes."

"You're not going to use any of that for this business, are you?"

"No. Absolutely not. That's where I draw the line."

"Good. Because that money is like a gift from Trevor to Natalie, and I don't want that to change."

I hadn't realized she'd felt so strongly about it, but as I thought about it, I understood. Her son was gone, and she'd allowed his child to be adopted by Marcus. Of course she wanted to feel like Trevor was contributing something to Natalie's future. "I understand."

"Thank you, Lily."

# Chapter Six

Over the next two months, Marcus, Jason, and Rick worked hard to get their business going and managed to sign several of their old clients to their new firm. Despite that, I knew it would probably be a while before they turned a profit. In the meantime, I had to dip into our savings to pay the bills, and I became more and more worried about how long it would be before we saw any new income.

"Our savings have nearly run out," I said to Marcus one evening after we'd put the children to bed. He leaned against the couch cushions and gazed at me, but didn't say anything. He'd been working so hard, and I hated to put further stress on him, but I had to ask, I had to know. My voice softened as I spoke. "When do you think you'll bring home a paycheck?"

His jaw tightened. "I don't know, Lily. It's hard to get a business off the ground."

"Maybe I should get a job. You know, to help us get by for a while."

He laughed once, then shook his head. "It wouldn't be worth it. The costs of day care would take any money you earned."

His laughter stung a bit, although I knew he was right. "What about web design?" Soon after I'd moved to California I'd begun a web design business, starting with building a website for *Billi's*, the boutique my friend Billi owned, and extending to other businesses in town. After I'd married Marcus and had become pregnant with Jackson, I'd helped my clients find someone else to maintain their websites, wanting to focus on my new family instead. Now I wished I'd kept it up.

"Wouldn't that take a lot of time?" Marcus asked.

I didn't know how much time it would take, and secretly worried how I would fit it in with taking care of an infant and a toddler, but I was getting desperate. "I can make it work."

Marcus rubbed the back of his neck. "It's up to you."

His lack of enthusiasm, combined with the stress I'd been feeling, pushed me to say the first thing that came to mind. "All I know is that we may not be able to pay the mortgage at the beginning of the month."

Marcus stared at me as if he was weighing whether to say something that had been on his mind. "I know you won't like this, but what about the money you put aside for Natalie? Isn't there, like, a hundred thousand dollars in that account?"

My heart skipped a beat as my fears that he would ask for money from Natalie's trust came to fruition. "We can't use that money, Marcus."

"Why not? It would just be a loan. You can even charge me interest."

I loved Marcus, and I didn't want to hurt him, but he had to hear the truth. "I already loaned you all the money I could."

He lifted his chin. "You say that like you don't think I'll be able to pay you back."

"Will you?" I shot back. "I'm not so sure anymore."

A blush rose on his face and he looked away from me before abruptly standing. "I'm going to bed."

I watched him leave the room, then stared at the wall across from me. Our conversation had gone nothing like I'd hoped. In fact, my worry had edged up several notches.

*Tomorrow I'll talk to Billi. Maybe she'll let me take over her website maintenance. I don't know if I'll earn much, but every little bit will help.*

As I waited for Marcus to fall asleep before going into the bedroom myself, my phone rang. It was Alyssa. We'd been talking every week or so as she'd kept me up-to-date on what was happening with her and Ty. After she'd stayed in her employer's hotel for over a week, Ty had come to realize she was serious about wanting him to change and he'd promised he would try. She'd moved back home and things had been going well ever since.

"I'm moving out," Alyssa said after a brief greeting.

"Why? What happened? I thought you guys had turned a corner."

"So did I, but last night Ty fell back into his old habits. He went gambling all night. When he came home this morning, he didn't even apologize. He just climbed into bed and fell asleep." She paused, then with a voice thick with tears, she said, "When I got home from work tonight, I told him I was moving out."

"What did he say?"

She dragged in a breath. "He said I should do whatever I thought was best."

"I'm so sorry." I thought about the fight I'd just had with Marcus and felt a kinship with Alyssa. Marriage was hard. My mother had died when I was quite young, so I had no memory of my parents' marriage and didn't know how they'd handled disagreements and trials. It was as if I was groping my way through a dark tunnel that had sharp sticks and large roots laid in my path. "Is there anything I can do to help?" I asked, although I had no more idea of what she should do than she did.

"It just helps to be able to talk to you."

"You know I'm always here to listen." *I can do that at least.*

We talked for a while longer, although I didn't tell her about my fight with Marcus.

*She has enough to worry about. Besides, I'm not ready to share my problems.*

---

When Marcus came home the next evening, he was smiling. Hopeful that meant he had good news, I immediately asked him what was going on.

"I came up with a solution," he said as he sat on the couch.

"A solution? To what?" There were many things that needed solving —how to pay our bills, how to repay the loan I'd given him, and especially how to restore the security I used to feel.

"Now, Lily, hear me out."

Alarm bells rang in my mind. If he already suspected I wouldn't like his "solution", then that was a bad sign.

"Come sit down," he said as Natalie climbed onto his lap.

I set Jackson on a blanket on the floor, then sat beside Marcus and looked at him expectantly.

He paused a moment. "We can move in with my parents."

"What?"

He held up his hand. "Please. Let me explain."

I clamped my mouth closed, but I already knew I wouldn't like what he would have to say.

"I figure we have three options. One, sell the house—"

My mouth flew open to protest, but he held up his hand. Fury blossomed inside me. *Who does he think he is making all these decisions for us without discussing it with me? This is* my *house. I* bought *it.*

Then I reminded myself that it was *our* house now. But still.

"If we were to sell the house," he continued, "we could use the proceeds to finance our needs." He smiled softly. "I know that's not an option, which is why I'm not suggesting it."

My pounding heart began slowing to its normal rate.

"The second option is to draw some of the equity out of the house and use that to finance our needs." He frowned. "I know you don't want us to go into debt, which is why I'm not suggesting that either."

I wanted to jump up and shout that this discussion would be unnecessary if he'd just gotten another job like a normal person, but I held myself in place and waited to hear the rest of his explanation. Jackson began fussing and I used the distraction as an opportunity to move off of the couch. My nerves were stretched tight, and I needed to think about something else, if only for a few seconds.

"Come here, baby," I murmured as I picked him up and cradled him against me. I stayed standing as I faced Marcus.

"So," Marcus said, dragging my attention back to him. "The obvious solution is to save on expenses by moving in with my parents."

The solution might have been obvious to him, but to me the obvious solution was for him to give up on this struggling business idea and work for somebody else—somebody who would give him a paycheck.

"Do you really think they'd be okay with that?" I doubted Trish would love having my children, not to mention Greta, at her house around the clock. Then I realized *that* was the solution. Trish would refuse—politely, of course—and then Marcus would be forced to come up with another idea. Perhaps I could even get him to think it was *his* idea for him to cut his losses and get a regular job.

"I already talked to them," Marcus said, shocking me out of my thoughts. "They're completely on board."

# Chapter Seven

—◁◆▷—

"Wait. What?" I asked, stunned that he'd gone forward with making arrangements without even discussing it with me first.

"That's right," he said. "Don't you see, Lily? If we don't have to pay the mortgage, that will save us a ton of money every month."

"I don't understand. If we keep the house, we'll still have to pay the mortgage."

"We can rent it out." Marcus looked away from me as if he didn't want to see my reaction.

"Rent it out?"

"Well, yeah. How else will we pay the mortgage?"

I didn't like it. Not at all. Not the idea of living with Marcus's parents, not the idea of renting out our home, and most certainly not the idea of all this upheaval.

"What do you think?"

I spoke without considering his reaction. "I think I'd prefer it if you just got a regular job. You know, one where somebody pays you every month."

He plopped Natalie on the couch beside him and jumped up to face me. "That's not going to happen, Lily."

"Why not?"

"Why not? You know why not." His jaw clenched as he looked away from me, then he met my gaze. "What about all the money you've already loaned me? Do you want to lose it all?"

"Of course not." I shifted Jackson to my other shoulder as a sheen of sweat broke out on my upper lip. I hated fighting with Marcus. We hardly ever fought.

*I guess we're overdue.*

Jackson began fussing, evidently feeling the tension in the room. Then Natalie began to whine.

"I hungry," she said.

"I need to take care of the kids," I said as I turned away from Marcus.

"Fine. I'll be in the bedroom."

I watched him go, my stomach churning.

"Mommy," Natalie said as she tugged on my jeans.

I looked down at her. "Okay, honey. Just a minute." In the kitchen I worked on autopilot, preparing dinner for our family like I did every night. When it was ready, I told Natalie to get daddy.

When he came in, he didn't look any happier than he'd looked when he'd left the room.

At dinner the children kept us distracted, allowing us to put off discussing the issue until they'd gone to bed. Once it was just the two of us, there was no more ignoring the problem.

"We need to figure this out, Lily," Marcus said as he got ready for bed.

I knew he was right, but that didn't make it any easier. All evening

I'd mulled over the idea of moving in with Marcus's parents and renting out our house. I didn't like it any better now than I had when he'd first proposed it, but over the last couple of hours I'd come to accept that there was not a better solution.

"Can we just have the renters sign a month to month agreement?" I asked.

Marcus looked at me in surprise. "So you'll do it?"

I sighed and folded my arms across my chest. "I don't know what else we can do." Unhappiness came through in my tone.

Marcus walked over to me and put his hands on my upper arms. "I know this isn't easy for you, Lily. And I promise I'll make things better." His voice softened. "I just need a little more time."

He kissed me and I let him enfold me in his arms. The fight was over. I wasn't thrilled with our decision, but at least a sense of peace had settled back over our home.

As I lay in bed, struggling to fall asleep, I turned to Marcus. "What do we have to do now?"

"I'll arrange for a storage place," he said as he looked at me. "For us to put our things in."

I hadn't even consider all the packing I would have to do. Overwhelmed by my new to-do list, any hint of sleep I'd begun to feel vanished. A short time later I heard Marcus softly snoring and I kind of resented it. Everything had gone the way he'd planned, but it seemed I was the one left to deal with the real work.

The next morning I began to rethink my agreement to move in with his parents.

*What if I can work it out so I can earn some money? Could we stay in our house then? How much would we need to get by?*

After feeding the children breakfast, I loaded them into my car and drove to *Billi's*, the boutique where I used to work, and my first web design client. I knew Billi often worked in the mornings, so I hoped I'd catch her there.

37

"Hello, Lily," she said when I walked through the door. She was arranging a display, but when she saw me she hurried over to give me a hug. "How are you?"

"I'm good. What about you? Your shop looks super cute, as usual."

"Thanks. Business is good." She reached out and touched Jackson's hand. "He's getting big."

"I know. Just like his father." Love for Marcus pulsed through me. He was such a good father to our children, and he was good to me. I wanted to support him, and talking to Billi was a first step in helping our family to potentially stay in our home.

"What brings you in today?"

I smiled nervously. "Actually, I was wondering how things are going with your website. I've decided to get back into web design, and you were the first one I thought of."

The happiness on her face dimmed. "I'm so sorry, Lily, but I just renewed my contract with my IT person."

"That's okay," I quickly said. "I just thought I'd check with you."

"If things don't work out with him, I'll definitely come to you."

"Thanks, Billi. I appreciate it."

We chatted for a few more minutes before I left. Discouraged that Billi didn't need my help, but not surprised, I again regretted stopping my business the year before.

With little hope, I spent the rest of the morning visiting the other business owners I'd worked with, but they all had the same response. I briefly considered trying to find new clients, but knew that would take time I just didn't have—taking care of my children truly was a full-time job.

Resigned to Marcus's solution, I drove home.

# Chapter Eight

"I posted an ad online to rent our house," Marcus said when he got home that night. "And I picked up boxes so we could start packing."

*Great.* The weight of all that I had to do settled over me, and a fresh bout of resentment set in. This wasn't a move to my newly purchased house like the last time I'd moved, so there was none of the excitement I'd felt before. In fact, I dreaded this move. Trish and I got along fine, but that didn't mean I wanted to share a house with her. Especially her house. I knew I would feel like a visitor. It would not be the same as being in my own house.

Yet I couldn't deny the generosity that she and Jeff were showing us. Even so, I felt like I was moving under protest.

"When are we making this move?" I asked Marcus.

"As soon as possible. That way we can get the house rented out."

I held back a sigh.

"What do you want to pack first?" Marcus asked.

I didn't want to pack anything at all, but I knew I had to get over that. "I don't know where to begin."

"How about the kitchen?" Marcus asked, not showing any anxiety about this move at all. "That's probably where we'll need to do the most packing."

"The kitchen? But I use it every day."

Marcus scrubbed his hands over his face. "What would you suggest then?"

Seeing Marcus get frustrated actually made me feel a little better. Now he was beginning to get an idea how *I* felt. "You'll need to pack all your tools. Why don't you start there?"

"Fine." He spun away from me and headed towards the garage.

I shook my head as I watched him go.

That weekend we worked hard, packing up the kitchen, the kids' rooms, and everything else we thought we could put in storage. Then Marcus and a friend of his hauled all of the boxes, along with our furniture, to the storage unit.

As I walked from empty room to empty room, sadness welled up inside me.

*When will we be able to come back to our home? What if we have to sell the house?*

That idea really depressed me.

Greta ran past me, enjoying the open space. Natalie giggled as Greta's tail swung in an arc and brushed against her face.

Now that we'd packed everything up, the house was ready to be rented. Marcus, knowing how unhappy I was with this whole thing, had offered to clean the house all by himself. I'd agreed without offering my help. Besides, someone had to take care of the children.

When Marcus and his buddy returned from their last trip to the storage unit, they loaded up everything we would take to his parents' house and headed over there. The children, Greta, and I were supposed to follow, but I lingered a few minutes longer, reluctant to leave.

"Where daddy go?" Natalie asked.

"He went to Grandma's house. We're going there too. Would you like that?"

She nodded, eagerness clear in her eyes.

I wished I was as excited as she was. With a final look around, I gathered the children and Greta and headed to my car.

When we pulled up to Jeff and Trish's house, Marcus and his buddy were busy carrying in our belongings. With Jackson in one arm and Greta's leash held in my hand, I led Natalie towards the front door.

Marcus's father Jeff was helping Marcus unload.

"Hello, Lily," Jeff said when he saw me. "Looks like you have your hands full." He set down the box he'd been carrying and came over to me, then reached for Jackson. "How about you let me hold this little guy?"

With gratitude, I handed him over.

He stared steadily into my eyes. "How are you dealing with all this?"

His sincere concern touched me and tears pushed against the backs of my eyes. I blinked a few times, forcing the tears away, before answering. "I appreciate you and Trish letting us move in. It's very generous of you."

"That's not what I asked," he said with a knowing smile.

I laughed. I'd always liked Jeff. When Trish had become hysterical at the news that Marcus wanted to marry me—a widow with a child—Jeff had remained calm and steady. "It wasn't my first choice," I said with a small smile.

"That's what I thought." He grinned. "You've always been quite independent, Lily. I'm sure this isn't easy for you." His eyes softened. "We appreciate you supporting Marcus in this venture of his." His lips quirked into a smile. "Despite the challenges."

"He's my husband. Of course I support him." I talked a good game, but Marcus knew how I really felt.

"Come on in," Jeff said. " Let's get you settled."

I followed him into the house, trying to keep Greta from jumping on everyone in her excitement at being in a new place. Did she remember this neighborhood? After all, we used to live right next door. Then I wondered who lived there now.

I headed toward the stairs, but Trish intercepted me.

"Let's put Greta outside," Trish said with a smile.

Trish kept her house immaculate. I wasn't sure how it was going to work to have two small children here, not to mention a dog.

*Just another issue for me to deal with.*

"Okay." I smiled in return to show I understood, then I led Greta outside where she immediately began exploring.

Trish's eyebrows pulled together as she watched Greta. "She's not going to dig up my flowers is she?"

I couldn't guarantee anything, but I wasn't about to tell Trish that. I was sure it would be difficult enough for her to have me and the children there without also worrying about my dog and what she might do to her yard.

We left Greta to explore as I mentally crossed my fingers that she wouldn't destroy anything on her first day here, then I took Jackson back from Jeff before following Trish upstairs.

"You and Marcus will be in here," Trish said as she pointed to one of her two guest rooms. "And the children will be in the other guest room."

I looked in both rooms and thought they looked fine, but they weren't home. Not wanting to think about our current situation, I turned to Trish with a question. "Who lives in my old house now?"

"It's a young couple with a baby. She's new to the area—kind of like you were when you moved here. I'm sure she'd love to make a new friend."

I decided I would stop by first thing Monday morning and

introduce myself. I could use the distraction. Besides, it would give me a good reason to get out of this house, at least for a while.

"No, Natalie," I said as she began jumping on the bed. "No monkeys jumping on the bed."

She giggled, but kept jumping.

"It's okay," Trish whispered. "She's too little to do any damage."

I looked at Trish in surprise. "Are you sure?"

"I want you to feel at home, Lily."

My surprise deepened, but I appreciated her welcoming attitude. "If she—" I gestured toward Natalie with my head. "If she gets to be too much, please let me know." I was moving here in protest, but for all I knew, Marcus had had to convince his parents to let us move in. Maybe Trish wasn't any more excited about it than I was.

"She's only two," Trish said with a smile. "I'm sure she'll be fine."

We spent the rest of the weekend getting settled, and I could tell it was going to be an adjustment—it seemed Marcus or I were constantly telling Natalie not to touch something or not to scream. Jeff and Trish kept smiles on their faces the whole time, but I could only imagine how they really felt.

At least Greta had behaved relatively well. She was used to being in the house with us, so she was unhappy when we wouldn't let her in as often as she wanted, but after a while she lay on the back porch with her head resting on her paws as she gazed at us through the glass door.

Seeing her there, and knowing what a wonderful dog she was, I wanted to protest and insist that she come inside with us. But it wasn't my house.

# Chapter Nine

Right after breakfast on Monday morning I loaded the children into the double stroller, then with Greta on her leash, we set out for a walk. I wanted to meet the woman who lived in my old house, but I was worried it was too early to knock on her door, so we strolled down the street for half an hour before turning back.

Greta seemed particularly happy to be out and about with us, and she sniffed everything within leash distance.

"Do you remember going on walks here, girl?" I asked as she stopped to inspect one particularly interesting bush. Jackson and Natalie were content to enjoy the scenery, and I wondered how long they would be content before I'd have to take them back to Jeff and Trish's house. It didn't feel like home yet—nowhere close to home—but it's where we lived. At least for now.

Over the weekend Marcus had been true to his word and had cleaned our house thoroughly, and had even shown it to a couple of people who had responded to the ad. As much as I wanted to move back home, I hoped we could rent our house quickly. At least that way we would get the money to pay the mortgage.

The sun warmed me as I headed back to Trish's house, and when I reached the driveway leading to my old house, I paused as I gazed at the place. It looked just like it had when I'd lived there, and after a moment, I wheeled the stroller up the drive. It was after nine, so I hoped the woman would be ready for a visitor.

As I approached the house, memories swam into my mind—good and bad—and I had to stop a moment to let them work their way through me.

A few moments later I knocked on the front door. It felt strange to have to knock, as I'd come through that door so many times in the past. Footsteps approached, and then the door opened. A woman in her twenties with auburn hair and sparkling green eyes greeted me, her face curious.

"Good morning," I said. Greta strained to go inside and I kept a tight grip on her leash. This was her first home, and the smells were familiar. "My name's Lily. I'm Jeff and Trish's daughter-in-law." With my free hand, I gestured in the direction of Marcus's parents' house. "We just moved in with them. Temporarily," I was quick to add. Then I smiled. "Trish said a woman my age lived here, so I thought I'd stop by and say hello."

A smile of pleasure curved her mouth. "I've heard about you. Trish told me you used to live here."

The welcoming look on her face warmed me. "Yes. About a year and a half ago."

"Would you like to come in?" Her gaze skimmed over Greta.

"If this is a good time, sure." I smiled. "If it's okay with you, perhaps Greta can go out back."

"That would be fine." She laughed. "She's probably familiar with the yard."

Pleased that she didn't object to my suggestion, my smile grew. "Yes, she certainly is."

"My name's Jordan, by the way."

I reached into the stroller to help the children out, and Jordan offered to take Greta's leash. After I set Natalie on the ground, I lifted Jackson out, then followed Jordan inside. Deja vu washed over me as I glanced around the familiar space. Besides the furniture being different, it looked pretty much the same as when I'd lived there.

We went out back where Jordan undid Greta's leash. Greta bounded away, off to explore her favorite places.

"Trish said you have a baby?" I said as I took the leash from her.

"Yes. Gabe is four months old. He'll probably wake up any time now."

We sat on the back porch, enjoying the pleasant morning as we chatted. Jordan had lived in the California Central Valley her entire life, but had moved into the house right after Gabe had been born.

"Does Mary still own the house?" I asked.

"Yes. She and her husband seem really nice."

"Did she tell you about the secret room?"

Jordan's eyebrows rose. "Secret room? I'm intrigued."

I laughed, pushing away the memory of the time I'd had to use it to hide from Trevor when he'd been searching for me and Natalie. "Yes. You get to it through the closet in the smaller bedroom."

"Oh! We should go check it out as soon as Gabe wakes up." She looked at me with wide eyes. "How did you discover it?"

"I was pregnant with Natalie," I said as I glanced at my two-year-old, who ran after Greta on the grass, "and when I was painting her closet, I noticed light around the edges of a small door. I managed to get the door open, and I found the room."

"Wow. That is so cool."

"Mary offered to change the doorway so that I could access it from the hall, but I told her not to worry about it." It was a good thing. I'd needed that secret room. "If you ask her, I'll bet she'd fix it for you so that you have another room."

"That would be nice. My husband has to work from home sometimes, so he'd probably like an office space."

A short time later her baby woke up. We left Greta in the backyard, but brought Natalie and Jackson inside while Jordan fed her baby. When she was done, she brought me up to Gabe's room.

"I'm dying to see this secret room, Lily."

I laughed at the excitement in her voice. With all the stress I'd felt lately, it had been a while since I'd enjoyed myself so much. I slid open the closet door, then pointed to the bottom right corner where the small door stood. "It's through there."

Jordan lay Gabe in his crib, then got on her hands and knees, moved the door aside, and crawled through. "Oh," she said, her voice clearly audible. "It's big in here." Then she coughed. "Although a bit dusty." A moment later she came back into Gabe's room. "I would definitely love to have the use of that room." She picked Gabe up from his crib and turned to me with a questioning look. "So you told Mary not to make the change?"

"It was just Natalie and me, so we didn't need the extra space." Her brow furrowed deeper, and I smiled. "It's a long story."

She smiled brightly. "I have lots of time." Genuine interest shone from her eyes.

Very few people knew my story, and I knew I'd have to get to know her better before I trusted her with it. I didn't want to offend her—I had a feeling we could be good friends—but I wasn't ready to launch into my crazy story just yet. "Maybe another time. These two will be getting hungry soon."

"You're welcome to stop by anytime," she said. "I love being home with this sweet baby, but it can get a little lonely too."

I knew exactly what she meant.

"And you can bring your dog too, if you'd like," she added.

I laughed. "I think Trish would appreciate having her house back to herself once in a while."

We walked down to the living room.

"How long do you think you'll be living with them?" Jordan asked.

That was a topic I didn't want to think about, but I answered her anyway. "Just until my husband can get his business off the ground."

"Oh. Well, for your sake, I hope it doesn't take too long."

I nodded vigorously. "Me too."

# Chapter Ten

That afternoon I sat in Trish's backyard talking to Alyssa on the phone while Jackson napped and Natalie played with her doll on the patio. Greta lay in the sun, enjoying the late spring day.

"Ty wants me to come home," Alyssa said.

"What do you want?"

"Of course I want to, but he doesn't think he's doing anything unreasonable." She sighed. "And as long as he has that attitude, I can't give in."

"What about counseling? Like a marriage counselor?"

"I suggested it, but he's resistant. He doesn't like the idea of talking about our problems with a stranger."

"Perhaps only time will get him to see that the path he's on is the wrong one," I said.

"You may be right, but it's hard to wait. I mean, should I continue renting one of these hotel rooms, or should I start to look for a more permanent place?"

The reality of Alyssa's situation hit me, and I was glad that even though I wasn't thrilled with our new living arrangements, at least Marcus and I were still together. "I think you should stay where you are. Don't give up hope yet."

"You're right. I guess I just needed to hear someone else say it."

---

That night when Marcus got home, Natalie ran to him and flung herself into his arms. "Daddy!" she said as he scooped her up.

We were in the living room, and Trish came in when she heard the commotion. Her face softened when she saw the sweet way Marcus interacted with Natalie, and I was glad. When Marcus had first suggested adopting Natalie, Trish had been reticent. Although Natalie's biological father was dead and Marcus had been in her life from the beginning, Trish had had some reservations, which Marcus had confided in me.

She'd worried that if our marriage failed, that he would be legally and financially tied to Natalie despite not being her biological father. Marcus had assured her that that was what he wanted, and that he loved Natalie as if she were his own. Eventually Trish had come to agree that adopting Natalie was the right thing, and she'd supported him completely.

Now, as Marcus set Natalie down and turned to me, I noticed how tired he looked. "How was your day?" I asked.

"Good," he said. "I got a lot of work done for one of our clients as well as creating a proposal for a prospective client." He smiled, then drew me into his arms. "But now that I'm home, my day has gotten much better."

Though I was glad he felt so at home here—the house he'd grown up in—I felt less so, and a tiny sliver of resentment lodged itself into my mind. My home was sitting empty, waiting for strangers to move in.

Exhaustion settled over me—besides the time I'd spent with Jordan and the time I'd spent in the backyard, I'd spent the day keeping Natalie's natural curiosity in check as she'd wandered from room to room.

I gazed at Marcus, then pushed aside my frustration with a smile. "I'm glad you're home too."

Marcus pulled away from me and looked at his mother, who stood nearby. "I'm starved."

Not that I necessarily enjoyed cooking, but usually when he came home from work hungry, he'd look to *me* for sustenance. I didn't like feeling so easily replaced, although I had to admit I was glad I wasn't the one responsible for every meal.

"I made beef stew," Trish said. "Your favorite."

"Mmm," Marcus said as he walked past me and toward his mother. "It smells delicious."

Trish's face lit up, and I felt guilty for my earlier resentment. Marcus was an only child, so of course his parents were thrilled to have him home for a while.

When Marcus and I finally had some time to ourselves that night, he confided that Rick, one of the men who'd started the business with him, had pulled out.

"He said the stress was putting too much strain on his marriage." Marcus gazed at me, a meaningful look in his eyes.

"I guess I can understand that." Our marriage was certainly feeling the strain, especially now that we'd had to give up our house. Half wishing Marcus would pull out too, and half proud of him for sticking with it, I said, "What will that mean for your business?"

"Well, we can't buy him out." He laughed, but it sounded tense. "We don't have enough cash to pay him back all at once, but we've agreed to pay him back gradually." Marcus sat on the foot of the bed as I stood in front of him. "He's going to work for another firm, which means it could be a potential conflict of interest for him to be invested in our firm, which is why we decided to start paying him back his share." His jaw tightened. "It also means he won't be able to help us find new clients."

"Is that going to cause a problem?"

Marcus sighed. "He was the one who had the most experience, and . . . well, he's the one who was the best at getting new clients."

Fresh worry bloomed inside me. What would this mean for their chances of success?

Evidently reading my mind, Marcus said, "This means it will probably take longer to get off the ground."

My heart sank. That meant we'd be living with Jeff and Trish that much longer. "What about other investors? Can you get more people to invest in your firm?"

He shook his head. "It's not that simple. The more people who invest, the more diluted my share will be, and the less control Jason and I will have."

"Oh."

"I just wanted you to know where things stand."

"I appreciate you telling me." I didn't add that I wished he would go work for another firm too. "Are you going to tell your parents? You know, since that probably means we'll be here longer."

"Not yet."

I itched to ask him how much longer we would need to stay here, but I knew that wouldn't be helpful. Besides, I knew he wouldn't have an answer for me.

# Chapter Eleven

Going to Jordan's house each morning became part of my daily routine. She enjoyed it as well, encouraging the children and me to come each day. She even liked having Greta come over.

Two weeks after I first met her I finally felt comfortable enough with her to tell her my story. We were on our daily walk when I told her how I'd had to flee from Trevor, and then how I'd had to lie to everyone about my identity.

"Wow," she said. "That's crazy, Lily. I never would have guessed that about you. You seem to have it all together."

I laughed quietly as we pushed our strollers. "It's been a long road. Having Marcus in my life has made all the difference."

"I know you don't love living with your in-laws, but I'm glad you live next door."

"I don't have a lot of girlfriends," I said as I thought about Alyssa.

We'd spoken the night before and she'd said she was still staying at the hotel, that Ty still refused to admit he had a problem. "Meeting you is one of the good things that's come from moving in with the Olivers."

"So what happened with Trevor?"

When I told her how Trevor had kidnapped Natalie when she was just a few weeks old, then had attempted to kill me, her eyes widened in shock. Then I recounted how Greta had saved me.

Her gaze shot to Greta, who walked steadily beside me. "Oh my gosh. That's insane."

"I know. I'm just grateful I have Natalie." I looked at Greta too as love for my loyal German Shepherd surged through me, and knew without her I would be dead.

"Wait," she said, her eyes wide. "Mary had mentioned that someone had once died in that house, but I had no idea it was . . . well, *your* husband."

"I'm so sorry, Jordan."

"*You're* sorry?" Her eyebrows rose. "What do you have to be sorry for? It wasn't your fault."

"I know. I just hope it doesn't upset you too much to know what happened in your house."

She shook her head. "No. That was in the past, and I try not to dwell on the past."

Relieved my story hadn't freaked her out, I nodded.

"I guess I'm lucky," she said. "My husband has always been good to me."

I'd only met her husband once, and he seemed like a nice man. "I didn't have the best judgment when it came to Trevor." I smiled. "But there's nothing I can do to change the that. The best part is, I have Natalie."

"You're amazing, Lily. You know that?"

What I had been through had never been my choice. Just because I'd survived it didn't mean I was amazing. At least I didn't think so.

"Thanks."

—◁◆▷—

When Marcus got home that evening, he finally had some good news.

"I think I've found renters for the house," he said as we sat down for dinner with his parents.

"Really?" I said.

"Yes. They look good on paper, they're only interested in a short-term agreement, and they seem like really nice people." He placed a serving of casserole on his plate then turned to me. "Do you want to meet them?"

"Yes." I definitely wanted to meet the people who could end up living in my home. And I hoped I wouldn't resent them.

"Great. They can meet us at the house at seven."

"We can watch the kids," Trish said.

She didn't offer to babysit often, so I was grateful. "Okay. That would be great."

As Marcus and I drove to our house, I pretended that we were going home. But that illusion was swiftly shattered when we pulled up to the house and found a couple with two school-aged children waiting for us on the porch.

"There they are," Marcus said.

Trying to put aside the sudden feeling of envy that they would be living in my house when I was stuck living with my in-laws, I climbed out of the car and plastered a smile to my mouth.

The woman, who looked like she was in her early thirties, approached me with a smile. "You must be Lily."

"Yes."

"This is Todd and Emily Barton," Marcus said.

We all shook hands as their children stood quietly by.

"Let's go inside," Marcus said, then he unlocked the door and ushered us in.

We chatted for ten minutes, then Marcus looked at me with a question in his eyes. I smiled slightly and gave an imperceptible nod.

"Well," Marcus said. "We'd love to have you live here."

I smiled gamely, but my stomach churned.

"That's wonderful," Emily said, then she looked right at me. "We'll take good care of your house."

I wondered if my reticence was written plainly on my face. "I'm sure you will."

They signed a month to month rental agreement. Now, if our situation changed, we would be able to move back in relatively quickly.

On the drive back to the Olivers' house, Marcus reached out and placed his hand on mine. "Thank you, Lily."

I wanted to tell him it was fine, but it really wasn't. I felt like I'd just given my home away. But then I looked at Marcus and saw the love in his eyes and knew that home was wherever he and our children were. "I know we'll move back some day."

"That's right. Eventually you'll see that all this sacrifice is worth it."

Intellectually I knew he was right, but emotionally I was struggling.

---

The next day I told Jordan the latest.

"Sounds like a good family will be living there" she said as she nursed Gabe.

I laughed, but it came out sounding discouraged. "I want *my* family to be living there."

"When you first moved in here," she said as she gestured to the room in which we sat, "I'll bet you never imagined that you would be happily married and have two children in such a short period of time."

That was for sure. When I'd moved in, my only hope had been that I could live in peace without Trevor tracking me down. Of course he had found me, but I'd survived, and Natalie had survived. "That's true."

"My point," she said with a smile, "is that you never know how things will work out."

"Yes, you never know what's around the corner. I just hope it's something good."

"Chances are it will be."

"Thanks," I said with a genuine smile. "I needed to hear that."

# Chapter Twelve

When the children, Greta, and I got back to the Olivers' house, Natalie seemed in especially high spirits, running around screaming, and then telling me no when I told her to stop. I set eight-month-old Jackson on the floor to practice crawling, and went to get Natalie.

"Those terrible twos," Trish said with a smile as she watched me wrestle Natalie to the floor to change her diaper.

I doubted she could remember Marcus going through them, but at least she understood Natalie was going through a normal stage.

The moment I released Natalie, she sprang up from the floor and took off, racing through the kitchen, then the dining room, and finally circling back through the living room. Then she ran directly to the base of the stairs.

"No, Natalie," I said as I hurried to keep her from climbing them. We didn't have stairs at our house, and I constantly worried that she would fall down these. I wanted to get a gate, but the idea that Jeff and Trish would have to go through a gate every time they wanted to go up or down their own stairs kept me from suggesting it. Instead I'd been extra-vigilant, keeping a constant eye on Natalie—which I needed to do anyway to keep her out of trouble.

Every night I fell into bed more exhausted than the day before. As accommodating as Jeff and Trish had been, their home just wasn't child-proofed to the extent I would have preferred.

"Let's play outside with Greta," I said to Natalie.

"Yay," she said as I picked her up. "Outside."

"Can you keep an eye on Jackson?" I asked Trish, then looked at Jackson, who was exploring the room.

"Why don't I come outside with you, and I can hold him?"

"Okay." Since we'd been living there, Trish and I had had several opportunities to visit, and though we'd been getting to know each other better, I still felt a barrier between us. It was as if she couldn't completely let her guard down and let me in. I hoped that over time she'd let me get to know the real Trish.

A short time later we were settled on the back patio, with Natalie running after Greta across the grassy yard.

"I love this time of year," Trish said.

I glanced at the clear blue of the early June sky and nodded my assent.

Trish looked at me with a smile. "I wanted to talk to you about something."

"Okay."

"I know you've been working hard to keep the bathroom your family is using clean, and to keep the kids' toys picked up, but I wanted to ask if you'd mind taking over some of the other chores. Like vacuuming the main floor and cleaning the downstairs half-bath."

"No, of course not. I'm happy to help. In fact I've been meaning to ask how I can help out more." Trying to manage the children in a new environment had been all I'd been able to handle up until that point, but I didn't like the idea that our presence was making more work for Trish. "What about dinners? I'd be happy to do the cooking some nights, or at least help you when you're cooking."

Trish laughed softly as she snuggled Jackson. "Just keeping these two entertained is job enough. Don't worry about meals, at least for now. Just the cleaning part would help me out."

"I can do that while the children are napping." Although I normally treasured that time to do something I enjoyed, like reading.

"Thank you. I appreciate it."

"Well, we really appreciate you letting us live here while Marcus gets things going."

"I'm sure he'll figure it out soon enough. Besides, he has his two partners to rely on."

I held back my look of surprise. It had been two weeks since Rick had pulled out of the business, but evidently Marcus had yet to tell his parents. I wasn't about to get in the middle of that, but wondered what Trish would think if she knew.

"Right," I said with a small smile.

"It seems you and the neighbor girl are getting on well."

"Yes, I really like Jordan. Her baby is only a few months younger than Jackson, so we have a lot in common."

"And she doesn't mind when you bring Greta over?" Trish's gaze strayed toward my German Shepherd, who lay in the sun.

"No, not at all."

"That's nice of her."

Thankfully Greta had left Trish's flowers alone, and after the first few days of seeing Greta sadly watching us from the sliding glass door, Trish had relented and said we could let Greta be in the house with us in the evenings—although during the day she preferred that Greta stay outside. Now she slept in our room like she always had, and she seemed perfectly happy in her new house.

Marcus got home late that night, after I'd already put the children to bed. He looked as exhausted as I felt, and when he sat beside me on the couch in the living room, I rubbed his shoulders.

"How'd it go today?" I asked.

"We signed a new client, so that's good."

"That's great," I said.

Jeff and Trish were in the other room, but after a few minutes they joined us.

"Marcus was just telling me that they got a new client today," I told them.

"That's good news," Jeff said. "Are they a big client?"

"They're one of our bigger clients, but my old firm had bigger ones."

"Well, one client at a time, right?" Jeff said.

"Exactly," Marcus said as he leaned back on the couch and tugged me against him.

I reveled in his closeness. It seemed I hardly saw him lately, and I missed him—another thing I didn't like about this new venture.

"How are things going with your partners?" Trish asked. "Are they pulling their weight?" She frowned slightly. "Are their working hours as long as yours?"

Marcus glanced at me, and I wondered if he knew I knew that his parents were unaware that Rick had pulled out.

"We're all working equally hard," he said.

I didn't say anything, but wondered why he didn't tell his parents the truth.

# Chapter Thirteen

"Surprise," I said when I walked into Marcus's office the next day with Jackson in my arms and Natalie right behind me.

He looked up from his desk, and when he saw our little group, his face lit up. "Hello," he said as he stood, a broad smile on his face. He leaned towards me for a kiss. "What a wonderful surprise."

I hugged him, glad to see how happy our appearance had made him. In all the time he'd been there, this was the first time I'd visited his office—partly because I didn't want to bother him when he was working and partly because I wasn't happy about the reality of our circumstances. But now I felt bad that it had taken me so long to stop by.

"What brings you here?" he asked.

I held up a large bag of food. "We wanted to have lunch with you."

He glanced at the computer monitor where a complicated program was visible. "I could use a break."

"What are you working on?"

He gestured toward the screen. "I'm designing an electrical system for one of our clients."

"Daddy," Natalie said as she pressed against his legs.

Marcus scooped her up. "Hey, sweetie. Did you come to have lunch with me?"

She nodded, her big blue eyes solemn.

"Okay then," he said as he glanced at me. "Let's eat."

We spread the blanket I'd brought onto his office floor, then set the food out and began eating.

"This brings back memories of when we were dating," Marcus said.

I laughed. "I don't remember a date on an office floor."

"Okay, maybe not *exactly* like our dates, but I've missed spending time with you."

I gazed at him, then nodded. "Me too."

Jackson crawled over to the garbage can and began pulling himself up, and I hurried over to keep him from crashing to the floor. Soon after, both the children became restless, so we packed up the remnants of our lunch, I kissed Marcus good-bye, and headed home, glad that I'd taken the time to go see him at work.

———— ◁◆▷ ————

"That Natalie is sure active," I overheard Trish say to Marcus a few days later. After helping me put the children down for the night, Marcus had gone downstairs to grab a glass of water, and I'd followed a short time later.

Marcus laughed. "She *is* two."

"I know that," Trish said with a tone of irritation. "But still, I wish Lily would get her under control. It's beginning to drive me crazy."

I paused in my approach to join them in the kitchen, wondering how Marcus would defend me.

"I'll talk to her," he said, not saying one word about how hard it was to care for a toddler and an infant in someone else's house.

Frustration ripped through me, but instead of bursting into the room to defend myself, I backed up and headed toward the room Marcus and I were using.

"Everything okay?" Jeff asked as he passed me in the hall.

"Yeah," I said as I pushed a smile onto my mouth. "Everything's fine." I wasn't about to complain to him about his wife. "I'm just tired."

"Okay. Well, good-night."

"Good-night." I decided reading in bed would make me feel better, so I pulled on a pair of comfy pajamas, then climbed under the sheets.

A short time later Marcus came into our room. "In bed already?"

"I'm pretty tired," I said, wanting to get a conversation about our children going. "Chasing our children around all day takes a lot out of me."

He sat on the edge of the bed beside me. "I'm sure it does." He gently stroked my face. "Have I told you lately how much I love you? And how much I appreciate all that you do for me and our children?"

Peacefulness washed over me at his loving words, and I opened my arms for an embrace. He drew me against him, and the frustration I'd been feeling melted away. "No," I said, "you haven't. I needed to hear that today."

He pulled away from me, a question on his face. "Oh? Why's that?"

*Honesty is the best policy.* "I overheard your mother complaining to you about the way I handle Natalie." My lips pressed together. "It kind of upset me."

"She's just not used to having children around all day." He laughed. "Remember, I was an only child. And a perfect one at that."

Despite myself, I laughed with him. "Perfect, huh?"

"That's the way I remember it."

"Uh-huh." A smile remained on my face. "I guess it would be hard to get used to having two little ones around."

"Thank you for understanding," Marcus said, then he stood and walked toward the adjoining bathroom.

*It would sure be nice if Natalie had a little friend to play with. That would keep her busy.*

Then I got an idea. My gaze went to Marcus as he got ready for bed, but I decided not to say anything about my idea until I'd nailed something down one way or the other.

---

The next morning during my daily walk with Jordan and our children, I asked her if she would watch Natalie and Jackson for an hour that morning.

"Sure," she said. "Mind telling me why?"

A smile grew on my face. "I'm going to apply for a job at the day care in town."

"What? Why?"

I tugged Greta's leash to keep her moving as we strolled along. "I was thinking how nice it would be if Natalie had some other children her age to play with. I can't afford to send her to preschool, and we can use the money from me getting a job, so I thought maybe I could work at the day care and bring Natalie and Jackson with me."

"That's a good idea."

"Do you think so? I haven't told Marcus yet."

"Why not?"

"I don't want him shooting down the idea before I've even tried."

"Why do you think he'd do that?"

"I don't think he wants me to get a job, but I want to know I can earn some income." I frowned. "I lived on my own and took care of myself, and then Natalie, for a long time before I married him."

She nodded. "Well, I'm happy to babysit for you while you go check it out."

"Thanks, Jordan."

# Chapter Fourteen

When I arrived at the day care, I took a deep breath and told myself that I was eminently qualified to work there. I was a mother of two small children, after all. I was in the trenches of motherhood. Besides, I loved children.

After being buzzed in by a worker, I told her why I was there.

"Let me have you speak to Cindy," she said with a smile. "She's the director."

I waited in the lobby and a moment later a woman I recognized came out.

"May I help you?" she asked, then a spark of recognition lit her eyes. "You used to work with Billi, right?"

"Yes." I held out my hand. "I'm Lily Oliver."

She shook my hand, then invited me in to her office. I explained why I was there, and she seemed interested.

"If we were to hire you," she said after we'd been talking for several minutes, "we would need to do a background check."

"That's fine." Even after all I'd been through with Trevor, I didn't think anything negative would appear on my record. "Would it work for me to bring my own children?"

"You mentioned that you'd need to. I don't have a problem with that, but be aware that you wouldn't spend much time with them while you're working."

"I understand." I didn't like the idea, but we desperately needed more income. In addition, Natalie would have the opportunity to play with other children.

"Let's go ahead and do the background check and have you do a TB test with your physician. If those both come back clean, I have a part-time opening that you could fill."

"Really?"

Cindy smiled. "Yes."

"That's great."

She handed me a form to fill out, which I quickly did, then told me she'd call me when the background check was complete. "I should get the results by early next week, which will give you plenty of time to complete the TB test."

We said our good-byes, and I drove to Jordan's.

"How did it go?" she asked.

"I think I've got a job." I held Jackson against me, wondering if I was making the right decision.

"Congratulations, Lily." Her eyebrows pulled together. "You don't sound super-enthusiastic though."

"It's just that I have mixed feelings about it. Plus I know I'm going to have to convince Marcus that it's a good idea."

"I'm sure it will work out."

I smiled, but I was much less certain. "I hope so."

Just as promised, by early the next week I heard back from Cindy.

The children were napping when my phone rang, and I was glad I was in my room where Trish wouldn't overhear my conversation.

"You passed the background check," Cindy said. "And I saw the TB test results you dropped by." She paused. "If you're still interested, we'd love to have you here."

"Yes," I said. "I'm still interested. When would you like me to start?"

"How about tomorrow?"

I hadn't told Marcus about the day care job yet—I'd been waiting to make sure everything went through first. But if I was going to start the next day, there would be no putting it off. "Sure. That sounds great."

"Wonderful. We'll see you tomorrow."

I would be working about five hours per day, which suited me just fine. It would give us some extra income, plus give Trish a break from the children.

Suddenly, I dreaded telling Marcus and his parents about my new job.

---

"I have some news," I said at dinner that evening. Everyone looked at me expectantly as my heart began to pound. "I got a job." I grinned nervously.

Marcus's hand froze as he lifted his fork to his mouth, then he tilted his head to the side. "What?"

"Where?" Trish asked.

"Congratulations, Lily," Jeff said.

"What about the children?" Marcus asked.

My gaze darted between the three of them, not sure who to address first, although I knew Marcus was the only one I really needed to answer to. My eyes met his. "I'll take them with me."

He slowly shook his head. "Wait. What kind of a job is this that you can take the children with you?"

"It's at a day care. And it's only part-time."

"A day care?" he asked. "What are you going to do there?"

Now he was just being dense. "Take care of the children, of course."

"What about *our* children? Who's going to take care of them while you're taking care of other people's?"

I didn't like having this argument in front of his parents, but it was my own fault for bringing it up at dinner. "Maybe we can talk about this later," I said.

"I want to talk about this now," he said.

"I've heard that day care workers who bring their own children to work hardly get to see their own children," Trish added.

I had no idea where she'd heard that, but I didn't appreciate her mentioning it now.

"You see?" Marcus said, as if his mother's comment was the end of the argument.

I knew she was right—Cindy had told me as much—but I didn't want Marcus to use that against me. I decided to go on the offensive, even though I knew it might hurt Marcus's ego. "We need the money."

His eyes darkened and his jaw clenched, then he glanced at his parents before meeting my gaze. When he spoke, his voice was low. "We're getting by, Lily."

"No," I said. "We're not. We haven't even contributed to the expenses here."

"That's okay," Jeff said. "We don't expect you to right now."

I turned to him with a look that begged for understanding. "But I don't like being dependent on you." I'd been taking care of myself for years, and I hated that I didn't have the means to do so now. This job would give us just enough money to help out with minimal expenses and have a little left over to put aside.

"I know," Jeff said. "But when we agreed to let your family move in, we understood it might be a little while before you could contribute financially."

"We appreciate that, Dad," Marcus said, then he looked at me. "You see, Lily? There's no need for you to go to work."

Without realizing it, I lifted my chin, then I said, "I'm starting tomorrow."

"What if I forbid it?" Marcus said, then his lips flattened

Memories of Trevor forbidding me to finish school, and then locking me in my own house flashed through my mind, and panic welled within me. As I spoke, my voice shook slightly. "I'm not asking for your permission."

Marcus's nostrils flared, then he threw his napkin on the table before storming out of the room.

"Why daddy mad?" Natalie asked before bursting into tears, obviously feeling the tension in the room. Then Jackson began fussing. I lifted him from his high chair and snuggled him on my lap.

Hot tears pushed into my eyes and I wondered if this job was worth it. But I didn't like being at the mercy of Marcus's lack of income, and I wanted to be able to support myself as I'd done before I'd ever met him. I'd liked that sense of independence, and I wanted to feel it again.

"I suppose you'll need me to keep an eye on Greta when you're gone," Trish said with a slight frown.

I hadn't even thought about that, and wondered if that's what would sabotage my plan. "If you wouldn't mind."

She smiled, but I could tell it was forced. "No, I'm sure it will be fine."

"Thank you." Jackson wouldn't stop fussing, so I stood and gently bounced him as I held him against my shoulder.

Natalie calmed down and continued eating her food. I wanted to talk to Marcus in private—although I also dreaded it—but I couldn't just walk away from Natalie.

"We can watch her," Jeff said, obviously sensing my dilemma.

"Thank you. I'll be back in a bit."

"No rush," he said with a warm smile—a smile so much like Marcus's that it pained me. Because I knew it might be a while before I saw the same smile on Marcus's face.

I nodded, then hurried to the stairs and up to our room.

# Chapter Fifteen

"Why would you go out and get a job without even discussing it with me first?" Marcus asked as he paced back and forth in our room.

I sat against the pillows on the bed as I held Jackson. "Because I knew you wouldn't want me to."

He stopped and stared at me. "Yet you did it anyway."

Feeling defensive, I went on the attack. "Now you know how I felt when you told me you'd already arranged for us to move in here before you'd ever mentioned it to me."

With eyebrows bunching, he said, "Is that what this is about? You're still angry with me for making you leave our house?"

I shook my head. "No. I mean yes, I'm still unhappy that we had to move, but that has nothing to do with me getting this job."

"Oh, really? Somehow I don't believe you."

He hadn't actually called me a liar, but it was uncomfortably close.

"Be honest, Marcus. We need the money."

His jaw clenched. "I know money's tight, but that doesn't make it okay for you to go behind my back and get a job that will affect our children."

"It will be good for them," I said. "Natalie has no one to play with right now. This way she'll have some children her age to play with."

He folded his arms across his chest. "What about Jackson? He's only eight months old. He doesn't need to play with other children."

"It won't hurt him to be around other babies. Besides, I'll be right there."

"No you won't. You'll be taking care of other people's children. Not ours."

I'd had about enough of his argument, and I decided to say what was really on my mind. "Look. If you find a job that brings in a steady paycheck, I'll quit at the day care."

Fury filled his eyes. "Is that what this is all about? Blackmail? If I don't do what you want then you'll go behind my back and . . ." He shook his head. "I know you hate living here, so what's next? You find someplace else to live, you take our children and change your name so I can't find you?" The expression in his eyes seemed to flatten. "Like you did to your first husband?"

My mouth fell open and it was as if someone was squeezing a vise around my chest. For a moment I couldn't speak, but when I found my voice, it came out in a whisper. "How dare you? How dare you blame me for getting myself—and my unborn child—out of an unsafe situation? I've apologized for lying to you about the fact that I was really married." I swallowed past the tightness in my throat. "I thought we'd gotten beyond that."

All at once Marcus's face seemed to sag. He walked around to the side of the bed closest to where I sat and knelt on the floor. "I'm sorry, Lily. That was uncalled for."

Still stung by what he obviously believed I was capable of, I wasn't so ready to forgive him. "Do you really think I'd do that to you?"

"No, of course not." He reached out to stroke my arm, but I pulled it out of his grasp.

"Then why would you say that to me?"

He clasped his hands together and rested them on the edge of the bed. "I'm stressed, I'm tired, and your announcement caught me off-guard." He frowned. "I know that's no excuse, but that's why I lashed out." His face softened. "I'm sorry, Lily. I know you would never do something like that to me."

But even as he spoke, a flicker of doubt crossed his face.

I gazed at him a moment. "I have a busy day ahead of me, and I'm tired. Would you please put Natalie to bed?"

Sadness filled his eyes. "Of course." Then he stood.

With Jackson in my arms, I pushed myself off of the bed. Marcus stood where I needed to go. "I'm going to put Jackson down."

"Sorry." He stepped aside and I passed him, then went into the room the children shared. After I put Jackson down, I got ready for bed, then climbed under the sheets. As I waited for Marcus to join me, my anger seeped away and I wanted to tell him I wasn't angry anymore, but I fell asleep before he ever came back into our room, and he left for work before I woke.

--------◁◆▷--------

When it was time to leave for my new job the next morning, Trish smiled and said, "Good luck. I'm sure you'll do great."

"Thanks." Then I smiled mischievously. "Enjoy the peace and quiet while we're gone."

She laughed. "Oh, I will."

At the day care, Natalie was less than thrilled to be left with strangers. With Jackson still in my arms, I knelt in front of her. "Mommy will be right next door, sweetie." I swept my arm toward the toys in the room. "Look at all the fun toys you can play with."

"Mommy stay here," she said as she sobbed and clung to my arm.

I hadn't bargained for this separation anxiety—on both our parts—but was grateful Marcus wasn't here to witness it. I could picture him standing with arms crossed and an "I told you so" expression on his face.

"It will be fine, Lily," Rochelle, the worker in the toddler room, told me as she gently unwound Natalie's fingers from my arm.

Once I was free, I smiled unsteadily at Natalie's tear-streaked face, then hurried from the room. "One down," I murmured, "and one to go." Then I went into the infant room where Jackson would stay.

Though he preferred me over anyone else, he ended up being perfectly happy to let Katherine, the worker for the infants' room, take him.

I was assigned to the preschoolers' room, primarily because my own children weren't in there, and I threw myself into playing with the children and helping out wherever I was needed. Occasionally I managed to peek in on Natalie and Jackson and saw that they were perfectly fine, which set my mind at ease.

At the end of my shift—which had flown by—Cindy pulled me aside. "How did your first day go?"

"Really well," I said.

"You're a natural with the children, and they seem quite comfortable with you."

"Thanks. They're all so adorable."

"I know. And I'm glad to hear you say that." She laughed. "I've had new workers nearly fall down from exhaustion after working a day here, but you don't seem all that tired."

I laughed. "What's exhausting is keeping my two entertained all day at my in-law's house." I grimaced. "Well, it's my house too, at least for now. But it's not the same as my own place."

She touched my arm. "I understand." With a smile, she said, "We'll see you tomorrow."

A short time later Natalie, Jackson, and I were headed back home.

# Chapter Sixteen

"What did you do today?" Marcus asked Natalie when he got home from work. He glanced at me with a small smile, then turned his attention to Natalie.

"I play with toys," she said excitedly.

"Oh, you did?"

"Yes."

"Did you make any new friends?"

She nodded happily, and again I was glad Marcus hadn't witnessed her near-meltdown when I'd had to initially leave her.

"That's good," he said, then he faced me. "How was your first day?"

"Great. And as you can see, the kids survived." I don't know why I was feeling so snarky, but I couldn't seem to help myself.

"I never said they wouldn't," he said.

"No. You just implied it."

"Well, if that's the impression you got," he said as he put his arms around me, "then I'm sorry. That's certainly not what I meant to say."

I leaned against him, relishing his warmth and strength despite my earlier snarkiness. "I'm sorry, Marcus. I don't know why I'm acting so childish."

He kissed me, then smiled. "It's okay. You've been a trooper through all of this, and I appreciate it."

While I'd outwardly been a trooper, inside I was still unhappy with our current housing arrangement. Not only that, but now I was spending half the day away from our children. True, it had been my choice—but it was a choice I'd felt I'd had to make.

I didn't reply to Marcus's comment, but instead asked, "How was your day?"

"Good." He smiled, though he looked tired.

"Are you enjoying this? You know, getting your own business off the ground?"

His smile faltered a bit. "It has its ups and downs. But I'm really looking forward to the ups."

He was trying so hard. Guilt sliced through me at the lukewarm support I'd been giving him. "At least the money I'll be earning will buy us more time," I said.

"You don't have to do that. You know that, right?"

"Do what?"

"Go to work. It's enough work to take care of our two rug rats, don't you think?"

"Oh, there's no doubt about that." I didn't want to argue with him any longer. "Are you hungry?"

"I'm always hungry." He glanced toward the kitchen. "Something smells delicious. Do you know what it is?"

"Your mom told me she had it handled, so I have no idea what she made." Though I preferred to be in my own kitchen, I had to admit that it was nice not to have to make dinner most nights.

Once we were all seated around the dining room table and had begun eating, I turned to Trish. "Did Greta behave for you today?" When I'd gotten home from work I'd immediately been busy with the children, and hadn't had a chance to ask her.

"I'm getting used to her," she said.

Trish had fed Greta for me when I'd lived next door and had gone on the Alaskan cruise, so it wasn't the first time she'd been responsible for her. Of course this was the first time she'd been responsible for Greta while Greta had been at her house.

I couldn't tell what Trish really thought, and hoped seeing to Greta's needs while I was gone wasn't too much trouble. "Well, I appreciate it." I smiled. "I'll bet you enjoyed the peace and quiet while we were gone."

Trish laughed. "It was certainly a lot more quiet than I've gotten used to lately, but I didn't mind it."

"Well, I for one," Jeff began, "enjoy having the extra action that the kids bring."

Though appreciative of his support, I laughed. "That's because you're gone all day."

"Yeah, Jeff," Trish said, then she smiled at me.

After Marcus and I had put the children to bed, Marcus told me he was going to tell his parents that Rick had bailed on him and Jason.

"Okay," I said, curious what had prompted him to tell them now.

"I just thought they should know," he said, apparently reading my mind.

"Why didn't you tell them sooner?"

A small frown pulled down the corners of his mouth. "I suppose I didn't want the news to make them doubt the potential success of my new firm." He gazed at me a moment, as if he was wondering if the news had made *me* doubt the potential success of his new firm.

I smiled. "I'm sure they'll be supportive."

He nodded, evidently satisfied with my response.

The four of us gathered in the living room, with me sitting beside

Marcus on the couch while his parents sat across from us.

"What's going on?" Trish asked after Marcus had invited her and Jeff to discuss something with us.

"I thought you should know that one of my partners—Rick— has decided to pull out of the firm."

"Oh?" Jeff said. "Why's that?"

"He said it was putting too much strain on his marriage."

Both Trish and Jeff's gaze slid to me before going back to Marcus.

"I'm sure it's stressful," Jeff said, then paused. "What does this mean for you?"

Marcus laughed. "One less person to make decisions."

"What about Jason?" Trish asked. "The other partner? Do you think he'll eventually pull out too?"

A shiver of worry slid up my spine at that idea. That was all we needed—for the entire business to fall on Marcus's shoulders.

"He seems just as committed as me," Marcus said.

"Are you willing to take money from investors?" Jeff asked as he rested his forearms on his thighs.

"We're not actively pursuing investors, but we're not opposed to it." His eyebrows creased. "Why? Do you know someone who'd like to invest?"

Jeff glanced at Trish before meeting Marcus's gaze. "We would."

"That's not necessary," Marcus immediately said.

Jeff laughed. "I know it's not necessary, and we're not doing it out of charity. We believe in you, Marcus. We're doing this so that our money will eventually grow." His voice lowered. "It's an investment."

Their sincere offer brought a fresh wave of guilt over me. I'd been reluctant to loan Marcus—my own husband—my money. And ever since I'd given it to him, I'd resented the fact that he wasn't brining home a paycheck, topped off by the fact that we'd had to sacrifice by letting complete strangers rent our house.

Now his parents were freely offering their hard-earned money because they believed in their son.

"That's very generous of you," Marcus said. "But I'd like to keep your offer in reserve for now, if that's all right."

"Of course," Jeff said. "Whatever you'd like to do."

When Marcus and I were alone in our room, I asked him why he hadn't taken his parents up on their offer.

"I don't want to risk their retirement funds on my business."

A rush of air left my lungs. "But you're okay with risking our future?"

"We're young. This is the time we can afford to take risks."

I couldn't believe what I was hearing, and any guilt I'd felt earlier for not being more supportive evaporated. "What if I don't want to take risks?"

"We're in this together, Lily."

"Honestly, I don't feel like I had a choice."

His neck stiffened. "We talked about this when I first lost my job and you said you would support this."

"Maybe I hadn't realized what you were really asking me."

"Well, it's a little late to change your mind now, isn't it?"

I thought about the partner who had left because the new business had put too much strain on his marriage. What would happen to the firm if Marcus left? Would Jason be able to carry it on his own? As much as I wished things were different, I decided I wouldn't suggest that Marcus leave the new business. That wouldn't be fair to the other partner, and it wouldn't be fair to Marcus.

Even if *our* marriage was under a lot of strain due to the business.

"Yes," I said. "It is too late to change my mind. You've gone too far to back out now."

"I'm glad to hear you say that," he said as he slowly smiled. "Because I need your support now more than ever."

"Do you at least agree that my new job will help?"

With obvious reluctance, he nodded. "I suppose."

At least I'd gotten one concession from him.

"As long as it doesn't adversely affect the children," he added.

I didn't want that either, but after only one day at the day care, it seemed like they would be fine. "Right," I said, thinking that as long as I was there with them, they would be fine.

# Chapter Seventeen

Two weeks later Jackson came down with a nasty bug.

"You'll need to leave him at home, Lily," Cindy told me when I got to work.

Natalie had been adjusting well and had happily told me good-bye when I'd dropped her off, but Jackson was fussy and feverish.

"I don't know if my mother-in-law is up for the challenge of caring for a sick child." Besides, I really didn't want to ask her.

Cindy frowned. "I suppose we can get by without you for a day or two until he's better, but you know our policy. If a child has a fever, he isn't welcome."

Evidently a child had come to the day care sick, otherwise Jackson wouldn't be sick now. I nodded. "Okay."

Cindy gave me an understanding smile, then walked away.

"I guess we're going home, sweetie-pie," I murmured against

Jackson's flushed cheek. He sagged against me, not interested in anything but being held.

When I went to get Natalie, she was busy playing and didn't want to leave.

"So typical," Rochelle said. "They get upset when Mom drops them off, and then get upset when Mom wants them to leave."

I laughed with her, but was glad Natalie enjoyed being there. Five minutes later I'd pried her away from the play kitchen and led her to our car. When we got home, Trish was surprised to see us.

"Jackson's sick," I said by way of explanation.

"Oh no," she said as she lay the back of her hand against his forehead. "Do you have any baby Tylenol?"

*If we were in our own home I'd have what I need.* "I think it's packed away in storage."

"Do you want me to run and get some?"

I considered asking Jordan if I could borrow some from her, but since the medication was dispensed with drops, I didn't want to use the same dispenser Gabe used. "If you wouldn't mind, that would be great."

Trish picked up her purse. "It's no problem. I'll be back in a jiffy."

---

By the time Marcus got home, Jackson had settled down, although he was obviously not feeling well.

"Is he okay?" Marcus asked as he held him. "When did he start getting sick?"

"I think he's got some sort of virus," I said.

"He caught it at that day care," Marcus said, his tone accusing.

"You don't know that. He could have caught something when we went to the grocery store."

"Come on, Lily. He's around other kids all day. Of course he got it there."

Though I knew he was probably right, I didn't like the way he was implying it was my fault. "Kids get sick. It's a natural part of childhood."

Trish walked into the living room where we were arguing.

"Lily's right, dear," she said. "Even you, as perfect as you were, got sick once in a while."

He frowned at his mother. "I just hate seeing him suffer like this."

"Of course you do." She stroked Jackson's chubby cheek. "No one wants to see him sick, but you can't change it now."

Late that night Jackson was fussier than ever, and when I picked him up from his crib, he rubbed his ear. "Oh no," I murmured. Natalie had only had a few ear infections in her short life, but Jackson had never had one.

I administered more Tylenol to Jackson, then rocked him until he fell asleep. Early the next morning Marcus woke me. Tired from being up with the baby during the night, I found it hard to open my eyes, but after a few moments I forced them open.

Marcus held Jackson in his arms, a worried look on his face. "I think he's really sick, Lily. Do you think you should take him to the doctor?"

Fairly certain he had an ear infection, I'd already planned on taking him first thing that morning. "You know we don't have health insurance, right?" I said.

When Marcus had lost his job, he'd lost his insurance along with it. We hadn't been able to afford the monthly insurance premiums, so we'd crossed our fingers and hoped nothing too expensive would happen.

"I don't care," he said. "You need to take him in."

"I know. I'm going to call the pediatrician as soon as they open." I pushed myself out of bed and held out my arms for my baby. "You need to go to work."

He seemed reluctant to hand him over, and I wondered if he thought I'd do something else to endanger our child, which irritated me. Finally, he relinquished him to me. "Will you let me know what the doctor says?"

"Yes," I said, "but I think it's just an ear infection."

"Oh."

It had been a while since Natalie had had one, and apparently Marcus had forgotten how common they were. "They'll give him antibiotics, and then he'll be fine."

"Okay." He kissed Jackson on the forehead, then kissed me on the lips. "I love you, Lily."

His tender words warmed me, especially after all the contention we'd been having lately. "I love you too."

After calling Cindy to let her know I wouldn't be coming in again, I made an appointment with the pediatrician. As it turned out, I was right. He had an ear infection.

I made sure to call Marcus and let him know the diagnosis.

"I'm glad it's just an infection," he said, then he paused. "I still think he got it from that day care."

I wasn't sure what he wanted me to say to that, so I stayed silent, hoping that would convey my unhappiness with his implied blame.

"Lily?"

"I'm here."

He sighed softly. "I've gotta go."

"Okay. See you when you get home."

"Bye." He hung up, and I did as well.

I stared at my phone, frustrated with Marcus and his attitude. A moment later Jackson reminded me that he wasn't feeling well as he began fussing.

# Chapter Eighteen

For the rest of the day, Jackson alternated between fussing and sleeping. Natalie, on the other hand, seemed completely happy to play with her dolls. I wanted to hang out with Jordan, but I knew she wouldn't appreciate exposing Gabe to a cold, so I kept the children entertained by taking them out back where the sun shone brightly, taking short walks around the neighborhood, and playing on the floor with them.

Jackson was a trooper, but I was glad when he slept.

"Can I fix you something to eat?" Trish asked as she poked her head into the family room where Natalie and I were building an elaborate structure out of blocks.

I looked up with a smile. "That would be really nice. Thanks." A moment later I stood and went to the entrance to the kitchen. "Can I help?"

Trish smiled at me. "That's okay. I've got it."

I went back into the family room to continue playing with Natalie and saw her knock over the tower she'd built. She giggled, and I laughed with her, realizing that I missed all the time I'd been able to spend with her before I started working.

*Maybe Marcus is right. Maybe working at the day care isn't the best thing for our family.*

I wasn't ready to admit that to him yet though.

---

The next morning Jackson seemed to feel quite a bit better. His fever was gone and he'd slept well the night before.

*It's back to work today.*

When the children and I arrived at the day care, Natalie had another near meltdown when I tried to leave her in the toddler room.

"What's the deal, Natalie?" I asked. "The other day you didn't want to leave."

She couldn't hear me through her tears as she clung to my leg. "Stay, Mommy," she cried.

I held back a sigh of exasperation. "I need to go to work, sweetheart."

Rochelle gently pried her from my leg. "She'll be fine, Lily."

Though I knew she was right, it wrenched my heart to see my baby girl so unhappy. "Thanks, Rochelle," I said as I hurried from the room.

I dropped Jackson off next, letting Katherine know that he was recovering from an ear infection. "He's on antibiotics, and he seems to be feeling a lot better." I kissed him on the forehead, then went to the preschooler's room.

When it was time to go home, I collected the children, and put them in their car seats, and when I climbed behind the wheel of my car, exhaustion settled over me and I realized I was beginning to hate my life. Tears pushed into my eyes, but I wiped them away impatiently, then turned on the engine and drove home.

After I put the children down for naps, I took out Trish's cleaning supplies and began cleaning the main floor of the house. As I worked, I thought about my life and tried to remember the good things in it. I had Marcus—a good man, a good husband, a good father. Even though we were having some challenges, I never doubted his love for me.

My mind went back over the years and I thought about Trevor—my first husband and Natalie's biological father. Though we'd loved each other in our own way, we'd had too many issues between us, and our relationship had been doomed to fail. I never felt that way with Marcus, and I knew that was huge.

I thought about how Trevor had tried to kill me. The sudden vivid memory of his hands wrapping around my throat, then squeezing as I'd begun to black out, shook me, and I had to stop what I was doing and look around, reassuring myself that it had happened a long time ago.

*You're still alive, Lily. You're still here. He's gone and he can't hurt you anymore.*

The image of Trevor lying on the floor of my living room with Greta's powerful jaws clamped around his throat filled my mind. It had been horrendous, but the only reason I'd survived was because of my loyal German Shepherd. And I adored her for it. She'd saved my life, and in the process, she'd saved Natalie's life.

I shuddered to think what Natalie's life would be like if I were dead and Trevor and his then-girlfriend, Amanda, were raising her. The idea horrified me.

I focused on the good things in my life as I finished scrubbing the sink in the half-bath.

A sudden crash, and then a scream, drew my attention away from my task, and I raced to the base of the stairs where I found Natalie lying in a heap, screaming in a high-pitched wail that told me she was in severe pain.

"Natalie," I whispered. "Oh my gosh, Natalie."

"What happened?" Trish said as she hurried to my side.

Natalie continued to wail as I looked her over.

"She must have fallen down the stairs," I said as I kept my focus on Natalie. "Where does it hurt, baby? Tell Mommy where it hurts, okay?"

"Hurts," she whimpered as she gingerly touched her right arm with her left hand.

I couldn't tell by looking, but I feared she'd broken her arm. Regardless, I knew I would need to take her to the hospital and have her checked out.

I turned to Trish. "Can you watch Jackson?"

"Of course."

With barely a nod in Trish's direction, I gently scooped Natalie into my arms, grabbed my purse from the table near the front door, and hurried out to the car.

Natalie continued to softly sob as I buckled her in her car seat.

"The doctor will fix it, okay, baby?"

Tears streamed down her face, but she didn't respond to my comment.

I jumped into the driver's seat and a moment later we were on our way to the hospital. Desperate to call Marcus, I waited until I was stopped at a light before I dialed his cell phone, but it went to voice mail.

"Hurts," Natalie cried out. "Hurts, Mommy."

Tears filled my eyes as helplessness swept over me, but I managed to leave Marcus a brief message before hanging up. A short time later we pulled up to the hospital and I rushed Natalie into the Emergency room.

Thankfully they weren't very busy and she was taken into an exam room almost immediately. Before long her arm was set, and she was feeling much better.

By the time we left, I still hadn't heard from Marcus, so I took

Natalie for some ice cream at the local ice cream shop. Halfway through eating our cones, Marcus called.

"Is she okay?" he asked the moment I said hello.

"Yes, she's fine now. We're having some ice cream downtown."

"I'm coming to meet you," he said.

"You don't need to. She's feeling much better now."

He hesitated. "Are you sure?"

"Yes, but thank you for offering." I paused. "Just come home when you can. I'm sure she'll want to show you her cast."

"A cast? Poor baby."

"I know." I recalled the horror of finding her at the bottom of the stairs, and unbidden, the thought came to me that if we were still in our house—which had no stairs—this never would have happened. I pushed down the comment that pressed against my tongue, and focused on the fact that Natalie was fine now.

"Okay," he said. "I'll come home as soon as I can."

We hung up, and when we got home I found Trish trying to comfort a fussy Jackson.

"I don't know if his ear is bothering him, or what," Trish said as she handed him to me, then she squatted in front of Natalie. "Oh my goodness, honey, look at your arm."

Natalie held out her cast, her eyes wide and her mouth turned down in a frown. "I have a owie."

"I see that." Trish picked her up and snuggled her close. "You poor thing." Then she turned to me. "We need to put up a gate on those stairs or something."

There was a hint of accusation in her tone, like why hadn't I suggested it before?

"I know," I said, leaving it at that. But I knew she was right. What kind of a mother was I that I was more concerned about the convenience of the adults in the house over the safety of my own child? Fresh tears fueled by the stress of the day filled my eyes, and I turned away. "I think he needs to be changed."

"Okay," Trish said. "I'll keep Natalie with me."

I nodded, but hurried up the stairs without replying, and once I got to my room, I let the tears fall.

*If we still lived in our house things would be different. I wouldn't be going to work each day, Jackson wouldn't be suffering with an ear infection, and most importantly, Natalie wouldn't have a broken arm. Why did I agree to let Marcus start his own business? What was I thinking?*

Tears overflowed my lashes and rolled down my cheeks.

# Chapter Nineteen

By the time Marcus got home, I'd gotten myself under control, although I was still pretty upset.

"How are you?" He asked as he pulled me into a warm embrace.

His parents were standing nearby, so I said I was fine. Instead, I waited until the children were in bed and we were alone in our room before I expressed my concerns.

"I was terrified when I saw Natalie at the bottom of the stairs," I said. "It was horrible."

"When I heard your message, I felt sick to my stomach." He gently stroked my arm. "I'm sorry I wasn't available when you called. I was in a meeting."

"That's okay. I handled it." I didn't blame him for not being available, but I did hold him partially responsible that it had even happened. "I . . . uh, I paid the bill with our credit card."

He frowned. "Okay." Then he switched gears. "My mom suggested that we put a gate at the top and the bottom of the stairs," he said. "We should have done that before this happened."

"I thought about it—" I let my sentence trail off.

"Why didn't you say anything then? If we'd had a gate installed this never would've happened."

I detected a tone of accusation in his voice—very similar to what I'd heard when Jackson had gotten sick. The stress I'd felt earlier came roaring back, and I spoke without thinking. "If we'd never moved here, this wouldn't have happened either. Did you ever think of that?"

He took a step back. "Are you saying this is my fault?"

"Are you saying it's mine?"

His lips compressed into a straight line. "I know what you're trying to say, and I'm tired of you saying it." His jaw tightened. "It's time for you to accept reality, Lily. We're living here now. You need to adjust to that."

Anger and frustration blossomed within me. "What if I don't want to adjust to that? Then what?"

He gazed at me a moment. "I'm not sure what you're saying."

I wasn't sure what I was saying either. All I knew was that I didn't want to be here anymore. And then I knew what I was going to do. "I'm going to take the kids to visit their grandparents in Las Vegas."

"What about your job?" His eyes narrowed, like he was happy that my job might not work out for me.

"Don't worry about that. It's *my* job, not yours."

"How long will you be gone?"

"I don't know yet. I'll have to see what works for Marcy, and I'll want to visit Alyssa too."

His head moved in a slight nod, then he broke our gaze. "I'm going downstairs for a while."

"Good night." I watched him leave, then I called Marcy, Trevor's mother.

"We'd love to have you come for a visit," she said after I explained what I wanted to do.

"When is a good time?"

"This weekend would be great."

I told her how Natalie had fallen and broken her arm. "I think it would be good to get away for a little while."

"You know you're always welcome here, Lily."

"Yes. And I really appreciate that." I hadn't talked to her in a while and we had a lot to catch up on. Marcy had always given me good advice, and I was counting on her to give me advice when I came to visit.

I called Alyssa next.

"I'm off on Monday," she said. "I'd love to spend the day with you."

We made arrangements for me to come to the hotel room where she was staying on Monday, then she told me there was no progress with Ty, and after chatting for a while longer, we hung up.

The next day at day care, everyone oohed and aahed over Natalie's broken arm. She smiled under all the attention, and with the Tylenol I had given her that morning, she seemed to feel okay.

After work I texted Jordan to see if she wanted to go on a walk. She did, and a short time later we were strolling down our street.

"I've missed our morning walks," she said.

"Me too." I got a better grip on Greta's leash, then smiled at Jordan. "It feels like my life has been crazy lately."

"Are you liking your new job?"

I shrugged. "I did at first, but now I'm not so sure."

"What don't you like about it?"

"I mostly miss the control over my time like I had before."

She laughed. "I don't feel like I have any control over my time." She pointed to Gabe in the stroller. "He's the one who makes my schedule."

I laughed with her. "I know what you mean, but at least you're spending your days with him."

"If you don't like it, is it possible for you to quit?"

I held back a grimace. "That would make Marcus happy."

Jordan looked at me sharply. "*You're* the one who has to work there each day. What makes *you* happy?"

"It's not only that. I made such a big deal about us needing the money I'm earning that I would look stupid if I were to quit now."

"Who cares if you look stupid? What's more important anyway? Your pride, or what's best for your children and you?"

Her words hit me hard. Was I letting my pride get in the way of what was best for my family? Or was working the right thing for me to do?

"I don't know what my problem is," I said. "Mothers of young children have to go to work every day." I laughed softly. "That's why the day care is needed in the first place."

Jordan tilted her head as she looked at me. "What does that have to do with you?"

"It's just that I feel kind of selfish and guilty for wanting to quit this job so I can be home with my children."

Jordan stopped and placed her hand on my arm, forcing me to stop. "Listen to yourself, Lily. That doesn't even make sense."

"What do you mean?" I asked as we started walking again.

"You feel guilty and selfish because you want to take care of your own children?"

I could see what she meant, and I didn't understand it myself. "Maybe it just feels wrong to be able to get what I want. Like, why am I so special?"

Jordan laughed and shook her head. "When Derek and I found out I was pregnant, it wasn't easy to decide that I would stay home with Gabe." She looked straight at me. "It's been a sacrifice for us, Lily. And

I don't feel guilty at all."

It would be a sacrifice for us too, I realized. We would basically have zero income, which I hated, but for right now that was okay.

Jordan glanced at me before speaking. "Every woman has to decide for herself what is best for her and her family—without guilt or worrying about what anyone else thinks of her decision." Her eyebrows rose. "That includes you."

She'd given me a lot to think about, and I appreciated her insight.

That afternoon as the children napped, I stayed in my room and thought about my conversation with Jordan. In a perfect world, we would be living in our house, Marcus would be bringing home a paycheck, and I wouldn't have to make this decision at all.

But we didn't live in a perfect world. Life was imperfect, and I had to learn to make hard choices. Though I knew this was something I should discuss with Marcus, I couldn't really see the point. I already knew what he wanted—he wanted me to quit. He hadn't wanted me to get the job in the first place.

No, this was a decision I would have to come to on my own.

# Chapter Twenty

The night before I left for Las Vegas, while Marcus and I were in the privacy of our room, he asked, "Are you going to visit Marcy and John because you want to see them? Or are you going there to get away from me?"

Truthfully, it was a little of both. There had been tension and strain between us ever since we'd moved in with his parents, and I just needed a little space. But I also hadn't seen the Caldwells in many months.

I didn't want to leave on a negative note, so I gave Marcus a half-true answer. "They haven't seen Natalie since Jackson was born." I smiled at him. "I think this visit is overdue."

A small frown formed on his mouth. "Okay." He paused. "When do you think you'll be back?"

I hadn't made a decision whether to quit my job at the day care or not, so I couldn't take off very much time. "I'll get there tomorrow,

Saturday, and I want to spend a couple of days there, plus I'm going to see Alyssa on Monday. So my plan is to come back on Tuesday."

"The people at the day care are okay with you taking two days off work?"

As I gazed at Marcus, an unexpected feeling of love for him blossomed inside me, and I almost told him that I was considering quitting my job, but decided to wait until I'd made my final decision—no point in saying one thing and then ending up doing another. "Yes," I said.

"Okay." He leaned towards me and pressed a kiss to my mouth. "Tell John and Marcy hello for me."

I nodded. "I will."

---

The drive to Vegas was long—seven hours—but Natalie and Jackson slept much of the way, making the drive bearable.

The moment Marcy opened the door and threw her arms around me, warmth and security flowed over me.

"It's so wonderful to see you," she said, then her gaze went to Natalie and Jackson. "And these two are as adorable as ever."

Natalie barely hesitated before letting Marcy take her out of my arms.

"Oh, she remembers me," Marcy said as we followed her inside.

I wasn't sure if it was that as much as the fact that spending time at the day care had made Natalie more comfortable with multiple people. In any case, it made Marcy happy, so that was good.

"Scott and Chris and their families are going to come over for dinner tomorrow," Marcy said as she carried Natalie into the living room where we sat on the couch.

"There they are," John said as he came into the room.

I stood and hugged him, overwhelmed with gratitude that Trevor's parents had become like surrogate parents to me. A moment later he took Jackson from my arms.

"He looks a lot like his daddy," John said.

I smiled as I thought of Marcus. "He sure does."

"Natalie," he said in a soft voice as he sat beside her and Marcy on the couch. "What happened to your arm?"

"I got a owie," she said with a small pout.

"Oh no." Then he smiled. "Can I draw a picture on your cast?"

Natalie giggled, then looked at me.

"It's okay," I said to her.

Her bright blue eyes—so much like Trevor's—went to John, who stood and said, "I'll be right back with a marker." He winked at me as he handed Jackson back to me.

Not for the first time, I wondered where I would be if Trevor had been more like his parents—kind and sweet.

*You wouldn't be with Marcus, which means you wouldn't have Jackson.*

That was something I couldn't begin to contemplate, and it emphasized that everything happened for a reason. I wouldn't be the person I'd become if I hadn't gone through all those terrible times with Trevor. They had been awful, but I didn't regret where I found myself now and the relationships I'd developed.

"Here we are," John said as he sat beside Natalie and began drawing on her cast.

Mesmerized, she held perfectly still as he drew a picture of a little girl that looked remarkably like Natalie.

"I didn't know you were such a good artist," I said, impressed with his skill.

He laughed, but I could tell my comment pleased him. "I like to draw once in a while."

"Draw Greta," Natalie said as she tapped on her cast.

John froze for a split second—so briefly that if I hadn't been watching for his reaction to the name of the dog that had killed his son, I wouldn't have noticed it at all.

"Okay," he finally said, but I noticed his hand shook a little.

John and Marcy had never met Greta, although they knew she was a German Shepherd. When they'd come for my formal wedding to Marcus, I'd put Greta in a doggie resort for the time they would be there, fearful that seeing her would be too hard on them.

John finished drawing a dog on Natalie's cast, and she smiled, clearly delighted. She slid off of the couch and ran over to show me what he'd done.

"I love it," I said with enthusiasm. I pointed to the drawing of the little girl. "She looks just like you."

Natalie nodded, then walked over to Marcy and showed her.

We relaxed for the rest of the evening, and after I put the children to bed, John left Marcy and me to visit on our own.

"Tell me what's going on in your life," Marcy said. "You mentioned that you're living at Jeff and Trish's place while Marcus gets his business off the ground. How's that going?"

"I hate it," I said, surprising myself with the vehemence in my voice.

"Hate it? Really? Why?"

At the look of surprise on Marcy's face, I quickly said, "Don't get me wrong. Trish and Jeff have been very nice about everything, but I miss having *my* house, where *I'm* the one in charge."

She nodded. "You feel like a guest who's overstayed her welcome."

"Kind of, yeah."

"I understand." She chuckled. "Having two women share one kitchen is always a challenge."

A small smile lifted one side of my mouth. "We don't exactly share the kitchen. Besides breakfast, Trish pretty much does all the cooking." I laughed. "Not that I mind—I've never loved to cook." My laughter died away. "But I'd like to have my own kitchen again."

"Of course you would." Her chin tilted downward as she gazed at me. "And you will, Lily."

"But?"

She smiled. "But . . . good things come to those who wait."

"I know, but it's the waiting that I don't like."

"You've always been a bit . . ." She tapped her chin. "Impulsive, I guess I'd say. Would you agree?"

I thought about the way Trevor and I had married so soon after we'd met—he'd pressured me, but still, I'd agreed. And then how I'd decided to get the job at the day care, and before I knew it, I was employed. "Yes. Sometimes."

Marcy's smile widened. "So you wouldn't exactly classify yourself as patient?"

This time I laughed with confidence. "No. That is definitely not a virtue I've mastered."

"Then maybe you can look at this time in your life as an advanced class on gaining patience."

"I suppose that's one way to see it," I said.

Marcy nodded as if she'd solved one of my problems. And maybe she had. Maybe I was just expecting too much, too soon.

"Tell me about this new job you mentioned," she said.

I told her all about it—how I'd thought we needed the money and how I'd thought it would give Natalie the opportunity to play with other children. "But Marcus didn't want me to do it."

Her eyebrows rose. "Yet you did it anyway?"

*She's from a different generation—one where a woman obeys her husband.* "I didn't like him telling me what to do."

She tilted her head. "I thought the two of you were partners in your marriage."

Not liking where this was going, I said, "We are."

"So you discussed it with him before you agreed to take the job?"

"Not exactly." Guilt swept over me. I hadn't said a word to Marcus about even considering getting the job until I'd been hired. It had been a done deal, and there had been no way I was going to let him talk me out of it.

"I don't mean to be blunt, Lily, but it doesn't sound like you're treating Marcus as an equal partner."

She was being blunt, but since she was sort of an outside party to everything, and because I knew she only had my best interests at heart, it was easier to take it from her.

A flush crept up my cheeks as the truth of her words settled over me, and I stared at my lap.

"Lily," she said, her voice soft.

I looked up and met her gaze.

"Don't feel too bad. You haven't been married that long." She laughed. "Looking back on my own first years of marriage, I wish I'd known then what I know now. I would have done a lot of things differently."

Somehow that made me feel better. "What can I do to fix it?"

"Well, I would say that when you get home you should sit down with that husband of yours and talk to him about what you're feeling."

"It's not like we haven't talked about this."

She tucked her legs under her. "What do you mean?"

"I've told him I'm not happy living at his parents' house."

"And what did he say to that?"

"That that's the way it is now, and that I need to get used to it." The anger and frustration I'd felt at our fight a few days before came rushing back. "It's like he's totally disregarding my feelings."

"Or maybe he knows he can't change anything right now, and he feels helpless to make you happy."

I sighed. "I've told him that I would be perfectly happy if he were to work for someone and bring home a regular paycheck."

"But he's trying to start his own firm. He can't do both."

"I know."

She straightened her shoulders. "I see. You want him to forget this whole entrepreneur thing he's doing, and have things go back to how they were. You want life to be comfortable and easy again."

*She understands.* "Yes. Exactly.

Her lips pursed. "You know that's not going to happen, don't you?"

Deep inside I did know it, but that didn't make it any easier to accept. I wanted to argue with her, but in all reality the argument needed to be with Marcus. I sighed. "Yes, I suppose I do."

She smiled. "Good. Then when you have your conversation with him, that's the place you can start from."

"What do you mean?"

"I mean, instead of suggesting that he change his career plans, you can talk to him about how you can help him reach his career goals." A soft smile lit her face. "And then you can talk about what you want, and how he can help you get there."

When she said it like that, it made so much sense, but I knew the actual conversation with Marcus wouldn't be so easy. It would require me to completely accept our situation, and deep inside, I still resisted it.

"What are you thinking, Lily?"

"That you're right, but I'm not happy about it." A wry smile turned up the corners of my mouth.

Marcy laughed. "You don't have to be happy about it, but that won't change reality. And I think you know, Lily, that you have it in you to change your attitude. I also think you know that your attitude has a very powerful impact on your entire family."

As I thought about it, I realized she was right again. When I got upset and frustrated, that led to Marcus becoming upset as well. Even the children would sense the tension, and then they would become fussy.

Having grown up without a mother, I guess I'd never really understood the critical role a mother's attitude had on the entire household. I appreciated Marcy's wisdom, and told her as much.

"That's one benefit of growing old," she said with a smile. "You learn a lot throughout your life, and then you feel obligated to share it with others." Her mouth shaped into a small smirk. "Whether those other people want to hear it or not."

I laughed. "I may not have wanted to hear it, but I *needed* to hear it."

"It sounds like you're willing to change. That's half the battle."

I thought about Alyssa and Ty, and how Ty seemed unwilling to change.

*Poor Alyssa. I'm glad I'll be able to see her on Monday.*

# Chapter Twenty-One

Sunday afternoon, when Trevor's brothers and their families came over for a barbecue, I truly enjoyed myself. It was a much different experience than when I'd visited for the first time after Trevor's death. Then, Chris, the middle brother and the one who looked so much like Trevor, had been angry with me and had silently blamed me for his brother's death. Now, though he wasn't as effusive towards me as Scott was, he was warming up to me.

"I have to admit," Chris said as he bounced Jackson on his knee, "this little guy is pretty cute."

"Just pretty cute?" I said with a smile. "I think adorable is a better word for him."

Chris's wife, Melody, leaned over her husband's shoulder. "I have to agree with Lily, hon."

I smiled at her, thankful for the role she'd played in helping her husband to begin to come around.

"I remember when Natalie was his age," Deena, Scott's wife said as she joined us. "And now look at her."

"I know," I said. "They grow so fast. I'm trying to enjoy every minute I have with them." Then it hit me. If I didn't have to work, why was I? I hadn't even been enjoying my job as much as I had at first. It would be one thing if I loved it, or if we needed the money—not that we couldn't use it, but Marcus and his parents had made it clear we could get by without it. If either of those reasons were in play, I could understand my stubbornness in keeping my job.

But neither was, so why was I insisting on keeping that job?

Was it simply to show Marcus that I was my own woman, to prove to him that he couldn't make decisions for me? He'd never shown any inclination to tell me what to do. Yes, he'd asked me not to take the job, but I'd completely disregarded what he wanted and had only focused on what I wanted.

And what did I want exactly? To show him that since he wasn't bringing home a paycheck, that I would do it instead? That would have been fine if we needed me to. But we didn't.

*I'm going to give my two weeks notice when I get home.*

The moment the thought clarified in my head, peace and relief cascaded over me, and I knew I'd made the right decision. Suddenly giddy, I found I couldn't sit still. And I wanted to share my decision with Marcy.

"I'm going to see if Marcy needs any help," I said as I stood. "Do you want me to take the baby?"

"I'll take him," Deena said before anyone else could offer.

I smiled at her, beyond grateful to have these people in my life—people who loved me and my children. "Thank you."

A few moments later I found Marcy tidying up in the kitchen.

"Would you like me to wash those pots?" I asked, pointing to the stack to the side of the sink.

"That would be great. I'll dry."

I filled the sink with hot, soapy water, and after washing and rinsing the first pot, I handed it to her. "I made a decision," I said, my heart light.

"Oh?"

"Yes. I'm going to quit my job."

She smiled. "Have you told Marcus?"

"No. I just decided a few minutes ago."

She nodded as she dried the next pot I handed her. "What made you change your mind?"

"I guess I realized that since I don't have to work, I'd rather spend the time with Natalie and Jackson. I mean, before I know it, they'll both be grown."

"That's truer than you realize, Lily. But the main thing is, if this decision is right for you and your family, then I'm happy for you."

"Thank you."

"Lily, you made it," Alyssa said as she let me into her room at the hotel.

Though her hair and make-up were perfect, she looked tired, and I could tell she'd lost weight.

"How are you?" I asked as I drew her into a hug.

"Not great, if you want to know the truth."

We sat on the small couch, and I curled my legs beneath me.

"It's so quiet without Natalie and Jackson," she said.

Marcy and John had volunteered to babysit, and I'd agreed, knowing there wouldn't be a lot for the kids to do while I visited with Alyssa. "I know. But it's nice for a change." I glanced around the small space. "Your room is cozy."

"What you're trying to say is 'small'," she said with a laugh. "But I've done what I can to make it feel more like home." Her chin quivered, then tears filled her eyes. "I want to go home, Lily. I want to be with Ty."

I reached out and rubbed her arm. "Have you talked to him lately?"

She nodded, then wiped the tears from her face. "I talked to him yesterday, and he told me he misses me." She inhaled through her nose, then slowly exhaled through her mouth. "He asked me to come home."

"Well, that's good. Right?"

"Yes, but when I talked to him about his gambling, he changed the subject."

I felt for her, but I knew from my experience with Trevor and the drinking he'd refused to give up, that she couldn't make him change. It would have to come from him. "Have you talked to him about seeing a marriage counselor?"

"I've suggested it a couple of times, and I think he's starting to warm to the idea."

I smiled. "It sounds like there's hope."

She nodded. "That's the only thing keeping me going right now."

We talked for a while longer, then we went to lunch. By the time I got back to Marcy and John's, I was emotionally wrung out. Compared to Alyssa and Ty's problems, mine seemed small. She had zero control over the outcome of her marriage, but my issue—dealing with my living situation and supporting Marcus—was completely in my hands.

Gratitude for that huge difference swept over me, and I knew I'd been selfish. In a hurry now to be with Marcus and to tell him how sorry I was, I was eager to head home the next day.

"Did they behave for you?" I asked Marcy as I took Jackson from her arms.

"Of course they did. We went to the park and had a picnic, then they both napped."

"I really appreciate you watching them. It made it a lot easier to visit with Alyssa."

"We don't get to see them very often, so we loved having them all to ourselves."

———◁◆▷———

Early the next morning we headed home. The drive seemed longer than it had on the way down, but that was because all three of us were ready to be home.

When we pulled up to the house in the early afternoon, I was surprised to see Marcus's car parked in the driveway. He was never home this early.

As I unloaded the children from the car, he came out to meet us.

"Marcus," I said when he stopped beside me. Eager to tell him my decision, and to tell him how sorry I was for my behavior, I smiled broadly.

A troubled expression filled his face, and a sense of foreboding surged through me. He lifted Jackson from his carseat, then he turned to me with a frown. "We need to talk."

# Chapter Twenty-Two

"What's wrong?" I asked as I stood beside the car.

"It's my mom," he said, his face somber.

My heart stuttered in alarm. "What happened? Is she all right?"

"No, she's not." A breath of air rushed from his mouth. "She has breast cancer."

I gasped, the news completely unexpected.

"Mommy," Natalie said from her car seat. "Get out."

"Just a minute, Natalie," I said with barely a glance, focusing back on Marcus. "What's going to happen now?"

"She's going to have surgery on Friday, and then she'll start chemo after that."

The severity of the situation settled over me. "How's she taking the news?"

A grimace played across Marcus's mouth. "Not well."

117

I remembered Marcus telling me how his mother had become hysterical when he'd told her he wanted to marry me. I liked Trish, and I'd gotten to know her a lot better since we'd moved in, but I also knew she could get extremely emotional—and overreact in the case of Marcus's announcement that he wanted to marry me.

"What can I do?" I asked, knowing I needed to be there for her, no matter what.

He rubbed the back of his neck with the hand not holding Jackson, then hesitated. "I know your job is important to you, and I respect that —"

I put my hand up, and his expression changed from uncertainty to annoyance. "Marcus, before you say anything else, you should know that I decided to quit my job."

"What? When did this happen?" His face relaxed. "Never mind. We can talk about that later. For now, I'm just relieved to hear that." He brushed his fingers along the curve of my cheek. "I know it's a lot to ask of you, but my mom will really need your help."

I placed my hand over his, loving the warmth of his strong hand against my skin. Peace and gratitude cascaded over me that I'd made the decision to quit my job on my own, and that now I would be available to step in and help where I was truly needed. "I'm happy to help."

A wry smile tugged at the corners of his mouth. "I'm not sure you know what you'll be getting yourself into."

I laughed. "You forget that I took care of my dad for two years starting when I was only eighteen."

Remembrance lit his eyes. "I had forgotten that." Then a chuckle burst from his mouth. "But this is my mother we're talking about, so it might be a little different."

I knew Trish, and I knew he wasn't exaggerating. Still, I knew I was up for it. Smiling, I nodded.

"Mommy," Natalie said again, this time with a strong edge of impatience.

"I'm sorry, baby." I freed her from her restraints and set her on the ground, then turned to Marcus. "Is it okay if we go inside now?"

He nodded. "Brace yourself."

The four of us trooped to the front door, and the moment we stepped inside, I heard weeping coming from the living room.

Trish's sobs were heart wrenching, and I immediately went to her side while Natalie stood beside Marcus in the entry. Jeff sat beside Trish, and I sat on the other side of her and wrapped my arms around her shoulders.

"Oh, Lily," she said, her voice cracking.

"I'm here," I said as the realization that she was as much a mother to me as Marcy was swept over me. I didn't want to lose her, and I knew I would do whatever I could to help her get through this.

My own mother had died when I was young, and though I didn't remember it, I had vague memories of the feelings of loss. And now, unexpectedly, they tore through me.

"It will be okay," I murmured, more to myself than to her.

Natalie ran to Trish and placed her hand on Trish's arm. "Grandma hurt?" A deep furrow formed between Natalie's eyes as she gazed into Trish's tear-streaked face.

The child-like concern shining from Natalie's face sent Trish into a fresh round of tears. She picked Natalie up and snuggled her, but after a moment she inhaled deeply, then exhaled slowly. "Grandma's okay," she whispered.

Jeff handed Trish a tissue, which she used to wipe the tears from her face, then she smiled at Natalie. "Did you have a good trip?"

Natalie gazed at Trish, evidently to make sure she really was okay, then she held up her cast and pointed to the pictures John had drawn.

"Who's that?" Trish asked, pointing to the image of the little girl.

"Natalie," Natalie said, then she pointed to the dog. "Greta."

"Can I draw something too?" Trish asked.

Natalie nodded, her eyes shiny with excitement.

"I'll get the markers," Marcus offered, and a moment later he handed a box to Trish.

"I like flowers," Trish said as she drew a bright blue flower on Natalie's cast. "Do you like it?"

"Yes," Natalie said, then she held out her arm for me to see.

"It's beautiful." I was glad Natalie had been able to take Trish's mind off of her sorrow, if only for a few minutes.

Natalie wriggled off of Trish's lap and ran directly to the sliding glass door where Greta was watching us. Natalie turned to us. "Greta inside."

"Not right now," I said, thinking Trish probably wasn't up for it.

"It's all right," Trish said, surprising me. Then she got up and opened the sliding glass door.

Greta bounded inside, obviously thrilled to see me and the children.

"You're a good girl," I said as I scratched her head. Her tail swung in a wide arc and her tongue lolled out. I smiled at Trish. "Thank you for taking care of her while we were gone."

"You're welcome," she said as she sat beside me.

Greta turned her attention to Trish, pressing her nose against Trish's hand. Trish pulled her hand away with a laugh that sounded forced.

"Come here, Greta," I said, knowing Trish didn't like wet dog noses against her skin.

"Lily has some news," Marcus said as he sat in the chair across from me.

All eyes moved to me, and I smiled nervously as I held on to Greta's collar. "I decided to quit my job."

At first no one spoke, then Trish said, "You don't have to do that."

*How to tell her I didn't do it for her?* "It must be serendipity, Trish, because I made the decision over the weekend." I smiled, and my voice softened. "Now I'll be home all day to help you with whatever you need."

Her eyes filled with tears. "I'm glad."

"That will be a big help," Jeff said, then he tilted his head. "What made you decide to quit?"

I explained how I'd come to the realization that what I wanted most was to be home with the children, and that since we could get by without me working right now, quitting was the right thing for me to do. "Maybe that will change at some point," I said. "But for now, this is what's best for our family."

"I agree," Marcus said.

I smiled at him, glad we were finally on the same page.

Marcus's cell phone rang, and after a brief conversation with the caller, he hung up and turned to me. "There's a problem at our house."

# Chapter Twenty-Three

"Who was on the phone?" I asked as all kinds of scenarios flooded my mind.

"Our renter. Todd Barton." Marcus frowned. "He said there was a fire in the kitchen."

"Oh no," I moaned as I closed my eyes.

"Nobody was injured."

*Why wasn't that the first thing I thought of?* "That's good, at least." I paused. "How bad is it?"

"I don't know. We should go over there and see."

*What else can go wrong today?*

"You can leave the kids with us," Jeff said.

I glanced at Trish. "Are you sure?"

"They'll just be in the way over there," she said with a smile. "Besides, I haven't seen them in days."

"Okay." I put Greta in the backyard, then Marcus and I walked out to his car.

"This is not good," he said as we drove to our house, his tone grave.

"Why do you say that?"

He glanced at me before focusing on the road. "If the damage is too extensive, the renters will have to move out, which means we won't have a way to pay the mortgage. Plus we'll need to pay the deductible to our insurance company."

My shoulders slumped as if someone had dropped a weight onto them.

Marcus grimaced. "This was something we really didn't need right now."

*None of this would have happened if we hadn't moved out.* But even as the thought came into my mind, I reminded myself that I was done going there. "We'll figure it out," I said instead.

Marcus put his hand on my leg. "Thank you, Lily."

"For what?"

He smiled at me. "For being positive." He sighed. "I've been feeling pretty overwhelmed with work, and now with my Mom's diagnosis, and then this . . ." He shook his head. "I'm glad you're on my side."

Shame and guilt swept over me that he would think for even a second that I wasn't on his side. We were a team—a partnership.

*Then you need to show it.* "I will always be on your side, Marcus."

He grasped my hand with his. "I know, and that means everything to me."

With my free hand, I covered our hands. "I love you, Marcus."

"I love you too." He smiled at me. "I'm glad you're home."

"Me too." Even with all of the challenges that lay ahead of us, at least we had each other. That, I knew, was the most important thing.

"Here we are," he said as we pulled up to our house.

"It looks okay from here," I said.

We walked to the front door together, then Marcus rang the bell. It felt weird to not be able to walk in, but I swallowed my pride as I waited for the Bartons to answer the door.

"Hello," Todd Barton said, his forehead deeply furrowed. "Come in."

The smell of stale smoke filled the air, and I walked directly into the kitchen. The wall behind the stove was black and covered with soot, the range vent was partially burned, and all the cabinets that surrounded the stove were blackened.

"What happened?" I asked as I stared at the damage.

Todd shifted from one foot to the other. "I guess one of the kids was making something to eat and left it on the stove." He cringed. "The fire department got here really fast though."

"I'm glad nobody got hurt," Marcus said.

"Me too," I was quick to add.

"I'm really sorry," Todd said.

Marcus half-smiled. "Accidents happen, right?"

"Especially with kids," Todd said.

I thought about Natalie falling down the stairs and breaking her arm just the week before, and wondered what other accidents awaited me.

"Yeah." Marcus glanced at the damage, then turned to Todd. "We'll need to fix this, obviously, but what will your family do while the stove is unusable?" He hesitated. "You're not planning on moving out, are you?"

Todd laughed. "We don't want to move, but I thought you'd be so mad that you'd kick us out."

I looked at Marcus, wondering if we *should* make them move out.

"I'm sure we can work something out," Marcus said.

I wondered what that meant, but decided to let him handle this.

"We can get by without the stove for a while," Todd said.

The garage door opened, and Todd's wife Emily walked in with their two children behind her. "I wondered who was here," she said, her face grim. "I'm so sorry about this."

*You said you'd take good care of my house.* I forced a smile on my face, trying not to think about the ruined tile backsplash that Marcus and I had so painstakingly installed. "Hi, Emily."

She looked at her husband, a question on her face.

"They said we can stay," he said.

Emily's head tilted back as she looked upward and released an audible sigh, then she looked right at me. "I promise, this won't happen again." A nervous laugh escaped her mouth. "Our kids have been banned from cooking."

*Good.*

"We'll call our insurance agent," Marcus said, "and get things moving to fix this."

"Thank you," Todd said.

Emily went to her husband's side. "Yes, thank you *so* much."

At the looks of gratitude on their faces, my annoyance lessened.

*What if something like this had happened when I'd been renting Mary's house and she had kicked me out? I would have been devastated. That place had become my home.*

On the drive back, Marcus showed his true feelings. "I wanted to kick them out."

I stared at him in surprise. "Then why didn't you?"

He shook his head and sighed. "Then we'd have to find new renters, and who knows how long that would take. At least they've been paying the rent on time."

"Yeah, that's great." I frowned. "As long as they don't burn the whole house down."

He laughed. "Yeah, that would suck."

---

At work the next day, I waited until Cindy had a free moment before I pulled her aside.

"I'm glad to have you back," she said as she pushed her hair behind her ear. "It's been kind of wild around here the last couple of days."

I glanced away, then met her gaze. "I'm really sorry to tell you this because I've truly appreciated the opportunity to work here—"

"No," she said with a frown. "Don't tell me."

"Yesterday I found out that my mother-in-law has breast cancer—"

"Oh, I'm so sorry."

I nodded. "She's going to need me more than ever, so I'm afraid I'm going to have to give up this job." I felt a little bad about using Trish's illness as an excuse to quit, but the reason didn't really matter anyway. The important thing was that I do what was best for my family.

"We'll miss you, Lily."

"Thank you." I hesitated. "I can give you two weeks' notice, if that would help."

"When does she start her treatment?"

"She's having surgery on Friday. I'm not sure how soon after that she'll start chemo."

"As much as we need you here, I think she needs you more right now, so don't worry about giving two weeks' notice." She grimaced. "But perhaps you can work tomorrow?"

"Of course. Her surgery isn't until the day after that, so that will be fine."

I finished out that day, and the next, and when it was time to leave the day care for the last time, I told everyone good-bye. I had enjoyed getting to know the other workers, and Natalie had liked playing with the other children, but I knew where I was needed now, and I was happy that I'd had the ability to make the choice that was right for me.

# Chapter Twenty-Four

On the day of Trish's surgery I stayed home with the children while Jeff and Marcus waited at the hospital. When Trish was in recovery, Marcus called.

"Surgery went well," he said. "They think they got it all, but she'll still need chemo and radiation."

"I hate that she's going through this," I said. "But I'm glad things are moving in the right direction. The important thing is that she gets better."

We talked for a few more minutes, then hung up.

Monday was the first day I was completely in charge of taking care of Trish, and as she rested on the couch, I knelt in front of her. "How are you feeling?"

"Tired."

"Your job right now is to rest," I said with a warm smile. "I'll take care of everything else, okay?"

She placed a hand on my arm. "You know, at first I wasn't sure about the four of you moving in here, but now I can't imagine it being any other way."

Surprised to hear her admit she'd had doubts, I nodded. "It was hard for me when we first moved in—I'd gotten used to having my own place."

Trish chuckled softly. "Yes, I could tell you weren't thrilled with this arrangement."

My face heated. *Was I that transparent?*

She smiled softly. "It's okay, Lily. I completely understood."

Cringing slightly, I said, "I'm past that now, and I'm glad I'm here to make your life easier while you go through this battle."

Tears filled her eyes. "You know, you're becoming the daughter I've always wished I had."

Deeply touched, I felt tears push against the backs of my eyes, and I put my arms around her, careful not to jostle her. When I drew back, I said, "You don't know how much that means to me."

Once Trish was settled, and I'd put the children down for naps, I called Alyssa to catch up.

"I can't believe all the things that have happened lately," she said after I'd told her about Trish's cancer and the fire at our house.

"I know. It's pretty crazy." I paused. "What about you and Ty? What's going on there?"

"I have some hopeful news."

Glad to hear something positive for a change, I said, "Oh, yeah? What's that?"

"We met with a marriage counselor the other day."

"That's great. How'd it go?"

"Not too bad. He stayed for the whole session, and he even answered the counselor's questions."

"That sounds extremely hopeful."

"I know." She paused. "If he keeps going to counseling, and the sessions are as productive as the first one, I think I'll be ready to move back home."

"I'm really glad to hear that."

"What about you?" she asked.

"What do you mean?"

"I mean, you quit your job so you could be with your children, and now you're going to be taking care of your mother-in-law. What are you going to do to take care of *you*?"

"I . . . I hadn't thought of that."

"Uh-huh. That's what I figured." She sighed. "Lily, if you ignore your own needs, you'll empty your tank pretty quickly and then you won't be any good to anyone."

"I'm sure I'll be fine." I laughed. "I've done this before."

"You mean when you took care of your father?"

"Yes, that's exactly what I mean."

"In case you've forgotten, you didn't have a husband and two children then."

I hadn't really considered that aspect. "That's true."

"Yes it is. So make sure and find something to do that's just about *you*, okay?"

I smiled, happy that Alyssa's marriage seemed to be on the right track, and glad that she was there for me, as she always had been. "All right."

"Good. Now tell me what cute things your kids have done lately."

I laughed, then launched into Natalie's latest antics.

---

By the time Marcus got home that night, I'd made dinner for the first time in a long time, and it felt great. Trish felt well enough to join us for dinner, although she hardly ate anything.

"I should have let you do some of the cooking before now," she said as she took a tiny bite of the casserole I'd made. "This is delicious."

"Thank you," I said. "I have to admit I've kind of missed cooking."

"You'll have plenty of time to make up for it now," Jeff said with a grin.

I knew Trish actually enjoyed cooking, and I decided I would make a special effort to include her whenever she felt up to it.

---

The next day while Trish napped, Jordan and I took our children and Greta on a long walk.

"It feels good to get out in the fresh air," I said as we strolled down the street.

"I've missed our walks," she said.

"I know. Life's just been so crazy lately."

She laughed. "For you, yes. For me it's been as boring as ever."

I missed having a boring life. I *liked* having a boring life. In fact, I wanted that life back—desperately—but I knew I had no control over the circumstances in which I found myself. "Enjoy it while it lasts," I said.

# Chapter Twenty-Five

As recommended by her doctor, Trish started her chemotherapy three weeks after her surgery. I'd easily fallen into the role of caretaker as Trish recovered from her surgery, and once she'd begun her chemo, I was grateful I had the skills necessary to make her life easier. I'd also taken on the responsibility of overseeing the repairs to our burned kitchen. Fortunately, once the workers had begun, it had only taken a week to complete the work, and they'd finished just before Trish had started her chemo.

After the first treatment it became clear that all of the duties of running the house would fall to me—cooking, cleaning, laundry, running errands that Jeff didn't have time for, caring for Trish's needs, caring for the children, taking Trish to her chemo treatments. The list seemed to go on and on, and after two months of being in charge, I was becoming exhausted.

In addition, when Trish was recovering from a treatment, I needed to keep the children occupied and quiet while she slept. Natalie had gotten her cast off, and was as inquisitive and busy as ever.

"Shhh, Natalie," I whispered when she screamed as Jackson reached for her doll. "Grandma Trish is sleeping."

"My doll," she said, only concerned about her favorite toy not getting into her baby brother's hands.

I held back a sigh, then went into the kitchen to start dinner, frequently checking on the children. Though they were happy, they were also making a big mess in the family room, spreading their toys all over the place. Knowing I would have to clean it up before dinner—it bothered Trish to have their toys everywhere and I didn't want her to have any extra stress—weariness swept over me. Trying not to think about all the tasks on my to-do list, I focused on the meal preparation as I thought about the break I would get when Marcus got home.

The children were always thrilled when he got home, and I was always thrilled to have their attention put onto another adult—one who could care for them without me worrying that the person was getting overwhelmed. Trish enjoyed the children too, but could only take them in small doses right now, and when Jeff was home he wanted to focus on Trish.

One of the highlights of my day was when Marcus got home. Not only because I loved him and wanted to spend time with him, but because he was such a great father.

---

By the time Jeff and Marcus got home that night, Trish was sitting on the couch in the living room and I had dinner ready. With Natalie in a booster seat and Jackson in his high chair, we all gathered around the table and began eating. I hadn't had a moment to talk to Marcus alone, so when he began talking about the latest goings-on at work, it was news to me.

"We signed a new client today," he said with a self-satisfied smile.

"That's fantastic," Jeff said. "It sounds like things are going really well."

Marcus glanced at me, before meeting his father's gaze. "Yes, but the only drawback is more work to do."

As I considered the implications, I frowned.

*I guess that means more work for me as well, and no break from caring for the children.*

I smiled at Marcus, but it was forced, and I missed our old life all the more. Resentment bubbled within me, but I forced it down as I reminded myself that I was going to be supportive of Marcus and not complain. He was working hard, and I appreciated that, but I was working hard too and I was starting to get burned out.

"Please excuse me," Trish said as she pushed back from the table. "I'm not feeling well."

Jeff jumped up to help her, escorting her into the living room to settle on the couch where she could be near us and lie down at the same time.

"Thank you for making dinner, Lily," Marcus said.

My lips curved into a pinched smile. "You're welcome."

For the rest of the meal I didn't add to the conversation between Marcus and Jeff, instead focusing on the children. When dinner was done, the men cleared the dishes while I loaded the dishwasher, and when the table was empty, Jeff took Natalie with him to be with Trish. Marcus kept Jackson entertained while still being with me in the kitchen as I worked.

I wanted to talk to Marcus about my concerns with his long hours, but I didn't want it to come across as complaining.

"Congratulations on your new client," I said to get the ball rolling.

"Thanks. Jason and I are pretty stoked about it."

In theory I was happy for them, but the effect of the additional work demands weighed on my mind. "At dinner you said this new client would mean more work." I set the glasses on the top rack of the dishwasher in a neat row, then looked at Marcus. "What does that mean exactly?"

He frowned. "A new client means an additional workload, and since we can't afford to hire anyone else yet, the workload will fall onto Jason and me."

I held back a sigh. "Does that mean we'll see less of you?"

His gaze remained steady on me. "Probably."

This time I couldn't keep the sigh inside, but I didn't say anything as I poured the dish detergent into the dishwasher, closed the door, and turned it on.

"I need you to support me, Lily."

Irritation ignited inside me. "Why would you say that? I *have* been supporting you."

Marcus's eyebrows rose. "I just get the sense that you're unhappy about this." His jaw tightened. "More clients equals the potential for more income."

*That's good at least.* "I know."

"I'm not sure that you do."

Aware that Marcus's parents weren't far away, I kept my voice low, although the irritation I felt at his condescending tone came through in my voice. "Of course I understand that. It's simple math."

"Then why do you seem angry about it?"

I glanced toward the doorway. "Can we discuss this later?"

With a small shake of his head, he said, "Yeah, sure." Then he turned and left.

I stared after him, frustrated that I couldn't speak freely without his parents overhearing.

*I want my own home again.*

The thought pounded into my head, and I squeezed my eyes closed for a moment. Of course I was glad to help Trish, but I didn't like the course my life had taken. Everything was in such upheaval—living in Marcus's parents' house, having to keep a tight rein on the children and the noise and mess they made, keeping my feelings tightly controlled, and hardly seeing my husband. All together it made for a stressful existence.

Yet admitting these things, even to myself, made me feel selfish, like I was ungrateful for the positive things in my life—good health, a caring husband, healthy children, in-laws who cared about me.

*Why do I feel unsatisfied?*

I didn't know, although I suspected it had to do with everything being outside of my control.

Despite the chaos and turmoil of hiding from Trevor, I'd had a fair amount of control over my life once I'd gotten away from him. And even after marrying Marcus I'd considered myself the captain of my own ship. But ever since he'd announced the loss of his job, I'd felt a sense of loss of control over my life, and I didn't like it.

I thought I'd already come to terms with the way things were now, but the more time I'd spent caring for Trish, the children, and the house, the more I'd begun to realize that simply telling Marcus I supported him wasn't the same as actually feeling that support. And now that he'd blithely announced he'd be working even more, I recognized how little I supported him, and how much I was beginning to resent this venture of his.

I just hoped I would be able to express my feelings without upsetting him and the delicate balance we'd been maintaining for the last number of weeks.

# Chapter Twenty-Six

"Okay, Lily. Tell me what's on your mind."

We'd gotten the children down for the night, and Marcus and I finally had some time alone.

I pulled the blankets back on our bed, sat on the sheets, and faced him. Not wanting to come off as selfish, but knowing that's exactly how I would sound, I hesitated.

He sat beside me and took my hands in his. With a soft voice, he said, "What you're doing for my mother is heroic. Do you know that?"

A small bit of air rushed from my nose as I gazed at him. *Heroic? You wouldn't think that if you knew how I'm really feeling.* "Thanks," I muttered, even more reluctant to share my thoughts.

"I know something's upsetting you." He chuckled softly. "I know you too well."

I couldn't help but smile, glad that my husband knew me well enough to read my mood. And to care about it—although I wasn't sure there was anything he could do to fix it. Guilt at my ingratitude surged through me, and I decided that the time wasn't right to tell him what I was feeling. What was the point? He couldn't do anything to fix it. We were all struggling with issues we had no control over—Trish with her cancer treatment, me with caring for everyone, Jeff with dealing with his wife's illness, Marcus trying to get a new business off the ground while trying to make his wife happy. What made me so special that my complaints had to be addressed *right this minute*?

"It's nothing," I said, this time managing to push a more genuine smile onto my mouth. "I'm just tired."

He laughed. "Aren't we all?"

*Exactly. Which is why I'm not going to burden you with my petty issues.* I nodded.

"Are you sure there's nothing you want to talk about?" he asked.

*I want my life back. I want to move back into our house. I want things to go back to how they were. I want you home at night, every night, at a predictable time. I want your mother to be well again.* As my list of wants raced through my mind, my smile faltered. "No."

Gazing at me as if he didn't believe me, his eyes softened. "You'd tell me if something was wrong, wouldn't you?"

*I don't know.* "Of course."

His lips curved in a satisfied smile. "Good."

---

Over the next two months, as Trish reached the end of her chemo treatments, I found myself at the breaking point. Many times I wanted to tell Marcus how overwhelmed I felt, but his plate was just as full as mine, and guilt at my selfishness silenced me.

Another challenge was our renters. They'd been saving for a down payment to buy their own house and had finally met their goal. They'd moved out two weeks before and Marcus had offered to head up the effort to find new renters. I'd wanted to suggest that maybe we could move back home, but we'd had enough friction between us without me bringing up the impossible, so I'd kept that idea to myself.

The one bright spot were the updates Alyssa gave me. She called regularly over the weeks to let me know the progress she and Ty were making in their counseling sessions. They were striving to work through their issues, and eventually they reached an important milestone.

"I moved back home," Alyssa told me in her latest call.

"That's wonderful." I talked softly as I sat on the couch and kept an eye on the children, not wanting to disturb Trish who was sleeping in her room.

"I know. I'm so happy, Lily. Ty hasn't been going to the casinos for a while now and he's rededicated himself to our marriage. The counseling really made a difference. We've both learned to communicate our feelings better, and to improve our listening."

Her joy came through in her voice, and it gave me hope that things would improve for me.

"I'm so glad to hear that."

"We've even come up with a plan on how to pay back the money he lost."

"Oh." I hadn't considered the long-term effects of his gambling.

"Yeah. It's awful that he lost so much money, but at least he's taking responsibility for it now."

"It sounds like things are back on track for you both."

"Yes. I couldn't be more pleased." She paused. "Tell me about your life. How's Trish doing?"

"She's worn out, but her spirits are good. Her last chemo treatment is later this week."

"Now *that's* good news."

"Yes. That's really lifted her spirits."

"What about you?" Alyssa asked. "How are you holding up?"

"I'm doing okay."

"What are you doing to take care of yourself?"

*Nothing. Who has time?* "You know. This and that."

"Come on, Lily. You're going to burn out if you don't take a break once in a while." She paused. "What about Marcus? Is he helping you out?"

Natalie grabbed a toy out of Jackson's hands, and he let out a wail.

An image of Marcus sitting at his desk with no screaming children to deal with filled my mind. "Natalie," I said as I gently took the toy away from her and gave it back to Jackson. "You need to share with your brother."

Then she began crying.

"I'm sorry, Alyssa. I've gotta go."

"Okay." She paused "Why don't you come for a visit?"

As fantastic as that sounded, I didn't see how I could get away. "I'd love to, but I don't know when I can."

"Just think about it."

"All right."

We hung up, and as I played peacemaker, I thought about Marcus and how little I seemed to see of him lately. As he'd predicted, he was busier than ever. He'd told me things were looking up, but in the day to day of things, it didn't seem to matter. It was almost as if I'd become a single mother again. But even when I'd actually been a single mother, he'd been around to help with Natalie much of the time. Now, though, it all fell on me. And that was on top of caring for Trish.

When the children were happily playing again, Jordan called.

"Are you up for a walk?"

I glanced out the window. The late Autumn day was brisk, but sunny. I smiled. "Absolutely."

A short time later I pushed the double stroller and held Greta's leash as Jordan walked beside me pushing Gabe.

"You called at just the right time," I said.

"Oh?"

"Yes. I've been needing to get out of the house, but it seems it's one thing after another that I need to do and before I know it the day is over."

"I've noticed you haven't been out walking as much lately."

"It's easy to let that slide," I said. "Especially with the days getting shorter."

"You have to make the time."

"Easier said than done."

Jordan stared at me a moment. "You sound stressed, Lily. Is there anything I can do to help?"

I frowned. "Thank you for asking, but there's really nothing anyone can do." *Although it would be nice if Marcus was home once in a while to play with our children. I think they miss him as much as I do.*

"Okay, but promise me you'll tell me if there's something I can do."

I considered asking her to babysit for me, but then I would feel obligated to return the favor, and that was just one more thing I couldn't add to my already overflowing plate. "I will."

We reached our usual turnaround point and headed back the way we'd come.

When the children, Greta, and I got home, Trish was sitting on the couch, her head wrapped in her favorite scarf.

"There you are," she said with a smile. "Did you have a nice walk?"

"Grandma," Natalie said as she climbed onto the couch beside her. "Read a book."

"How are you feeling?" I asked. "Can I get you anything?"

Trish laughed. "Maybe a book for me to read to Natalie."

I set Jackson on the floor, put Greta out back, then gathered several of Natalie's favorite books and brought them to Trish.

While Trish read to Natalie, and Jackson held onto the edge of the couch as he practiced walking, I prepared lunch.

"I can't tell you how happy I am to only have one treatment left,"

143

Trish said as we sat at the table.

I smiled. "It will be fantastic to have that behind you."

Her eyes closed briefly. "Yes." Then her gaze met mine. "And then we can get on with our lives."

I wondered what that meant exactly. How would my life change? Or would it? Marcus would still be gone much of the time, we would still be living at his parents' house, and I would still be unhappy.

# Chapter Twenty-Seven

"Today was your mom's last chemo treatment," I said to Marcus a few days later as I lay in bed while he sat propped against a pillow, reading.

"I know." Despite looking tired, he still seemed as happy as he did each day when he got home—unlike me, who was exhausted and worn down by the end of each day. Each night he still had enough energy to read in bed before going to sleep, while I was eager for the peaceful release of sleep.

"How is it that you manage to stay awake and read each night?" I asked as I gazed up at him, trying to keep the resentment from my voice.

He chuckled. "I guess I need some time to wind down at the end of the day."

"Wind down," I echoed. I wished I could wind down, but by the time I got the children to bed, all I wanted to do was climb into my own bed.

He smiled at me. "Yes. After working all day I need some time to decompress."

My jaw tightened as I tried to frame the words that insisted on being spoken. "It would sure be nice if you could make some time to play with your children." I was sure my eyes were practically sparking. "Maybe that would help you decompress."

With a frown, he set his book on the bed beside him. "I would, except by the time I get home you're putting them to bed."

I pushed myself up so I was facing him straight on. "I'm not going to keep them up past their bedtime so they can play with you."

"Why not? What's so critical about them going to bed at exactly eight o'clock each night? It's not like they have to get up for school the next day."

My heart pounded as the confrontation I'd been holding back for weeks came to the fore. "This will be news to you, but even if they get to bed late they still get up at the same time the next day, and guess what?" My eyebrows rose. "Then they'll be whiny and grumpy the next day." I frowned. "Again, this will be news to you, but that's hard to deal with."

Spots of color blossomed on his cheeks. "If it's anything like the way you're acting now, then I can only imagine how unpleasant that would be."

I tilted my head as fury roared to life. "Are you saying I'm being whiny and grumpy?"

He gazed at me a moment, as if deciding if he should go there. Then he did. "Yeah. You kind of are."

"You're saying I'm being childish." It came out as a statement. When he didn't respond, I spoke with a touch of bitterness. "What happened to me being heroic?"

"You have been, but I don't know where this other stuff's coming from."

"This other 'stuff', as you call it, is coming from the fact that I'm tired of being a single parent."

"A single parent?" He ran his hands through his hair. "Is that what you consider yourself?"

I could see my statement had upset him, but he had to hear the truth. "When I'm the only one caring for our children, then yes, that kind of makes me a single parent."

"Wow, Lily." He looked away and shook his head before meeting my gaze. "I don't even know how to respond to that."

"How about by saying that you'll *be* here well before the children's bedtime. Maybe you could even give them a bath and put them to bed once in a while." My next words came out as nearly a whisper. "I could sure use the break."

His mouth hung open. "Do you have any idea how hard I'm working?" With a sigh, he added, "I need you to support me, Lily."

"You know, you keep saying that. But I have yet to hear you offer to support *me*."

"Support you? I *am* supporting you. That's what going to work each day is all about."

Echoes of Trevor filled my mind, and my hands dampened with sweat. A memory burned inside me. A memory of him telling me that what I'd chosen to do—focus on my education—was selfish and that I should get a job instead of leaving the support of our family all on him. A memory that reminded me that his early attitude had only been a hint of his true self—abusive and controlling.

Would Marcus become like Trevor? Fear crawled up my spine at the thought, and as much as I knew Marcus was nothing like Trevor, I couldn't shake the feeling of unease that swept over me.

My lips were stiff as I spoke. "I'm sorry we're such a burden on you."

With a slight flinch, Marcus's eyes widened. "A burden? Why would you think that? You're not a burden. You're my responsibility."

I wasn't convinced. "What's the difference? Either way, without us you'd have a lot more freedom, a lot more flexibility to follow your dreams."

His head tilted at a questioning angle, and his lips parted in confusion. "What's the point of following my dreams if you're not there to share them with me? You and the children."

"But that's just it, Marcus. We're not sharing anything with you. How can we when you're never around?"

His jaw clenched as he gazed at me. "I just can't win, can I?"

"Is that what this is about?" I asked, even as I knew I was being unreasonable. "Winning?"

His breath came out in a rush. "You know that's not what I meant."

"What do you mean, then?"

His nostrils flared. "I mean there's just no pleasing you."

I knew what would please me, but we'd gone there too many times already, and I knew it was pointless to bring it up again. I looked away from him as my thoughts raced, then I turned back to face him. "I need some time away."

"What?"

I nodded. "When I talked to Alyssa the other day, she invited me to come for a visit." I gazed at him a moment. "I'm going to accept her offer."

He stared at me as if thinking through all the ramifications.

"I won't go until your mom's feeling better," I added.

"Okay." A small smile softened his face. "I think that's a good idea."

"You do?"

He reached out and stroked my face. "Yes I know how hard you've been working, Lily. You've earned some time away."

Knowing I would get the break I'd been craving, sudden lightness sweep over me. "Thank you, Marcus."

He frowned. "Why are you thanking me? I didn't do anything."

"Thank you for supporting me in this."

"Oh." His mouth curved into a smile as his eyebrows rose. "So now

I'm supporting you?"

My smile matched his. "Evidently, yes."

"I'm glad I'm finally doing something right."

I knew I'd been hard on him—and him agreeing that I should go visit Alyssa didn't change the fact that he was hardly around—but I was grateful that he hadn't argued with me. And I knew he was nothing like Trevor. I leaned toward him and kissed him on the mouth.

"I've missed that," he said as he drew me into his arms.

With my head cocked to the side, I said, "I've been here every night. You're the one who's been MIA."

He nodded slowly, his eyes on mine. "I see how it is."

I wasn't sure what he meant, but he didn't seem upset, and as I snuggled against his chest, hope grew within me that just maybe we'd taken the first step on the path to getting our relationship back on track.

# Chapter Twenty-Eight

The closer the children and I got to Vegas and Alyssa's house, the more relaxed I became. When I'd left home, Trish had been feeling well enough to take care of herself while Jeff and Marcus were at work, and had been glad that I had the opportunity to take some time for myself.

"You deserve it, Lily," she'd said as I'd fed the children breakfast. "I'll never be able to properly thank you for all you've done for me." Her smile had faltered as her eyes had filled with tears. "I'm so grateful that you're in my life."

Her sweet words had touched me and I'd reconsidered leaving. "Thank you, Trish. That means a lot to me." I smiled at her, and she must have sensed my reticence in leaving.

"I'll be fine." Then she'd motioned to Greta to come to her side and had begun scratching her head. "I'll have this little lady to keep me company."

Now, as I pulled up to Alyssa's house and took the children out of their carseats, I softly laughed, pleased that Trish had taken such a liking to Greta.

"Let's go see Aunt Alyssa," I said as I held Natalie's hand while balancing Jackson on my hip. The setting sun cast shadows across us as we walked up the driveway, and a few moments later Alyssa opened the front door.

"Lily," she said with a wide smile. "It's so good to see you."

My smile matched hers as we embraced, then she invited us in. I hadn't been to her house before, and I glanced around, taking in the contemporary style that she and Ty had chosen.

"Lily," Ty said as he walked towards us. "How are you?"

After all the heartache Alyssa had been through so recently because of Ty, I couldn't help but look at him more closely. With a head of thick brown hair, sparkling green eyes, and an attractive goatee, he looked just as I remembered him from their wedding. But I sensed something different about him. I hoped it was simply his change of heart toward Alyssa and their marriage.

When I saw him slip his hand into Alyssa's, then saw the joy on her face, I smiled, happy for them. But their affection also made me miss Marcus, and I felt bad about the tension we'd been experiencing lately.

*We'll figure it out.*

"Are you hungry after your long drive?" Alyssa asked. "I was about to make some tacos."

"That sounds great," I said.

We followed Alyssa into the kitchen, and after helping Natalie sit at the table with a snack, I began feeding Jackson while Alyssa browned a pan of ground beef.

"Do you need any help?" Ty asked Alyssa.

She smiled at him. "No, I've got it."

He glanced at me. "I'll leave you two to catch up then." A few moments later I heard sounds coming from the TV in the other room.

"I'm glad to see you so happy," I said.

A peaceful smile curved Alyssa's mouth. "When I came out to see you earlier this year, it was hard to imagine Ty and I would get to this point. But now that we're here, I can't imagine even considering giving up."

I couldn't imagine giving up on Marcus, and I was grateful neither one of us had ever suggested such a thing, despite the challenges we'd been facing. And I vowed to keep it that way.

Alyssa drained the drippings from the meat, set the pan back on the stove, then turned to me with a secret smile.

"What?" I asked.

She glanced toward the other room, then whispered. "We've decided to have a baby."

My eyebrows rose. "Are you pregnant?"

Her smile grew. "Not yet, but I hope I will be soon."

"That's great, Alyssa."

She nodded, then her gaze went to Natalie and Jackson before resting on me. "I'll expect lots of advice from you."

Laughing, I said, "And I'll be happy to give it."

At dinner, Ty and Alyssa were genuinely sweet with each other, which seemed to confirm Alyssa's assessment about the direction their relationship had taken. I could only hope Marcus and I would be in a similar place soon. Unfortunately, with all the friction we'd had between us lately, it was hard to imagine.

After I put the children down for the night, Ty, Alyssa, and I sat in the living room.

Ty settled into the couch next to Alyssa, and with a slight frown, said, "I guess Alyssa told you about my gambling problem."

My heart skipped a beat. *Is this going to be awkward?* I glanced at Alyssa before meeting Ty's gaze. "Uh, yeah."

He laughed. "It's okay. I'm glad she had you to talk to."

Relieved he wasn't uncomfortable with me knowing the struggle he'd gone through, I smiled. "We all have our challenges." Then I thought about mine, and my smile vanished.

"Ain't that the truth?" Alyssa said with a shake of her head.

Forcing my focus back on them, I pushed a smile onto my face as I nodded.

"I'm just glad Alyssa didn't give up on me," Ty said, then he shook his head. "I'd probably be sitting in a casino right now, gambling away every penny I had."

"You're worth the trouble," Alyssa said as she smiled at him.

I thought about Marcus and how frustrated I'd been with him lately. *Is he worth the trouble?* I imagined my life without him and knew he absolutely was. *Prove it, then. Show him he's worth it.* I thought about how I could show him how important he was to me and our children, and wished he was sitting beside me at that very moment.

*Maybe I should go home in the morning. But Marcus will be at work all day, so that would be pointless. Besides, I've already promised Marcy and John that I'd spend a couple of days with them. No, what I need to do is give Marcus the space he needs to do his job—without trying to make him feel guilty. It's a sacrifice to be the sole caretaker of our children, but being gone so much can't be easy on him either. I need to cut him some slack.*

"Are you okay, Lily?" Alyssa asked after no one had spoken for several minutes.

Realizing I'd been twisting my hands in my lap, I looked up and met her gaze. "Yeah." I smiled. "I'm fine." And I was. I knew it was time for me to be there for Marcus one hundred percent. And even though I would prefer to be living in my house again, in all reality I knew that it wasn't the place I was living that mattered, but rather the people I was with. That's what made it a home.

---

"I know you have challenges of your own, Lily," Alyssa said as I loaded the children into my car as I prepared to leave the next morning. "But you'll get through them."

I latched Jackson's car seat, then stood and smiled at Alyssa. "I know I will."

"I'm glad you were able to come for a visit."

"Me too." A smile of anticipation curved my mouth. "I'll come when your baby's born too."

She laughed. "That could be a while."

"I hope not. It would be fun if our kids were close in age."

"I know, right?"

I pulled her into a hug, then climbed into my car, and with a final wave, headed to John and Marcy's house.

---

"Lily!" Marcy said. "Hello."

Her warm welcome wrapped around me like a familiar soft blanket, and peace and comfort swept over me. I'd become close to Trish over the last several months, and I knew I was blessed to have these two women in my life.

"Grandma," Natalie squealed, much to Marcy's obvious joy.

Marcy scooped Natalie up and carried her inside, and Jackson and I followed.

"John's running an errand, but he should be back soon," she said.

I set Jackson down, and he immediately crawled to the couch then pulled himself up and started cruising along the edge.

"Look at him," Marcy said. "He'll be walking soon."

I laughed. "I know. And then I'll have to chase both him *and* Natalie."

Marcy set out crayons and a coloring book for Natalie, then we sat on the couch to catch up.

"How's Trish?" she asked.

I gave her an update, then added, "She was in really good spirits when I left."

"What about you?" she asked. "How are you doing? Are you taking care of yourself?"

I shrugged. "That's what this visit is about. Taking some time for myself."

Her eyes sparkled like she had a secret. "Good."

Curious to know if she was hiding something, but unsure how to ask, I didn't say anything.

"What are you coloring, Natalie?" she asked.

Natalie held up the picture of the princess she was coloring. "Princess."

"It's beautiful," I said.

I heard the door that led from the garage into the kitchen open.

"John's back," Marcy said with a wide smile.

I wondered where he'd been that seemed to excite her so much.

She jumped up, then turned to me. "Wait here."

Confused, I nodded. "Okay." I watched her leave.

"Where Grandma go?" Natalie asked.

"I don't know, sweetheart." I picked Jackson up and set him on my lap. Voices came from the other room, and I stood, ready to see what was going on. Then I remembered Marcy's explicit instructions to *wait here*, and sat back down.

When footsteps approached a moment later, my gaze went to the doorway.

"Marcus," I nearly squealed when I saw him standing on the threshold to the living room.

# Chapter Twenty-Nine

"Surprise," Marcus said as a triumphant smile curved his mouth.

I leapt from the couch, and with Jackson in my arms, I went into his embrace. A moment later I pulled away with a smile. "What are you doing here?"

Marcy and John walked up behind him.

"You were at the airport," I said to John. "Right?"

"That's right." A smug smile lifted the corners of his mouth.

My gaze went from John to Marcy, then stopped on Marcus. "You all planned this together."

He laughed. "Yes, we did. And it worked." With a satisfied smile, he said, "I can tell you had no clue I was coming."

Pleased by his unexpected appearance, I grinned. "Of course not. Why would I?" My eyes narrowed. "Wait a minute. What about work? Are you leaving it all on Jason?"

"Yes, I am. He's taking some time off in a couple of weeks, so it's all good."

Jackson held out his arms to Marcus. Still unsure what Marcus's arrival meant, I handed Jackson to him.

"How's my boy?" he said to Jackson, who smiled, clearly thrilled to see his daddy.

Not wanting to be left out, Natalie raced to Marcus's side. "Look, Daddy," she said as she held up her masterpiece.

Marcus squatted beside her. "Oh, Natalie. It's beautiful."

She beamed under his praise.

"So," I began with a tentative smile, "why are you here?"

Marcus laughed, then kissed me softly on the lips. "To take you away, my love."

Excitement and joy surged through me. "What?"

He chuckled at my response. "John and Marcy have graciously offered to babysit so you and I can take a couple of days to ourselves."

My gaze went to Marcy, who smiled broadly.

*So that's why she looked like she had a secret.*

"Thank you," I said.

"It's our pleasure," John said.

After transferring the car seats into John and Marcy's car, Marcus loaded the luggage he'd brought, along with my suitcase, into the trunk of my car.

"Call if you need anything," he said to Marcy.

"I'm sure we'll be fine," she reassured him.

We said our good-byes, then Marcus helped me into the passenger seat before climbing behind the wheel. "Are you ready?" he asked.

I gazed at my sweet husband. "If you're there, I'm ready."

He laughed, then started the car and pulled away from the curb.

"Where are we going?" I asked.

"I booked a hotel in town." He glanced at me with a knowing smile. "I knew you wouldn't want to be too far from Natalie and Jackson."

"You know me too well," I said with a laugh.

"That I do."

"What other surprises do you have up your sleeve."

A wide grin curved his mouth and set his eyes to twinkling. "You'll just have to wait and see."

More curious than ever, I settled into my seat and enjoyed the anticipation. A short time later we pulled up to one of the nicer hotels on the strip. A valet helped us out, then after taking our luggage out of the trunk and placing it on a cart, he drove away with our car.

Marcus checked us in, and a few minutes later he held open the door to our suite.

I walked across the marble floor, down the few steps into the living area, and stopped in front of the window that had an expansive view of the golf course below.

"This place is amazing," I said as I turned to Marcus.

A pleased smile filled his face. "I'm glad you like it."

My eyebrows pulled together. "Isn't it expensive though?"

With a chuckle, he said, "Let's not talk about money right now, okay?"

I didn't like the way he brushed off my concern—lack of money was one of our biggest problems. But I didn't want to ruin his plans with an argument right off the bat. "All right." Forcing a smile onto my mouth, I said, "What do you want to talk about?"

He drew me against him. "How about how much I've missed you?"

Remembering how much I'd missed him the night before when I'd chatted with Ty and Alyssa, I said, "I've missed you too. In fact, I was thinking about coming home today."

His eyebrows rose. "Oh yeah? Why didn't you?"

I laughed. "Because I'd promised Marcy and John that I'd come for a visit. It's a good thing, I guess. I wonder how she would have convinced me to stay if I'd told her I wasn't coming."

"I'm sure she would've come up with something."

I nodded. "How's your mom doing?"

"She's doing fine. Dad's been taking good care of her while you've been gone."

"Was she in on your little surprise?"

He laughed. "Yes."

---

We spent the next two days reconnecting—something our relationship desperately needed. For the last few months we'd hardly spent any quality time together, and being able to focus solely on each other renewed our feelings of love like nothing else could have.

"I'm sorry I've given you such a hard time," I said on our last day together.

Marcus brushed a stray piece of hair away from my face as we sat on the couch in our room, enjoying the view. "What do you mean?"

"I mean, I'm sorry I told you I feel like a single mother."

He grimaced. "You shouldn't feel sorry about that. After all, it's true." A soft sigh slipped from his mouth. "I know I've been working crazy-long hours for a while now, but it's going to change."

Not sure if I believed him, I frowned. "What if you get a new client? One that requires lots of your time?"

"We hired a new employee to help with the load."

I sat up straighter. "When? What about the cost?"

"He started a couple of weeks ago, and we can afford him."

Confused, my eyebrows bunched. "So you're making money now?"

He grinned. "Things are definitely looking up."

He'd alluded to that recently, and I was thrilled to hear he'd managed to hire more help. "That's great."

"Yes, it's a big relief."

I wanted to ask if he was doing well enough for us to move back into our house, but then I remembered my decision to prove to him that he was worth any sacrifice I had to make, and that I wouldn't lay any guilt on him for doing what he needed to do to support our family. He was working so hard. I needed to make sure he knew I appreciated it—despite the added stress it put on me.

"Marcus," I began.

He gazed at me. "Yes?"

"I want you to know how much it means to me to see you working so hard."

A soft smile lit his face. "I only do it because I love you and our children so much."

I stroked the rough skin on his cheek. "I know. That's why I wanted to tell you thank you. I know it's hard on you to be away from home so much."

He nodded. "That's right. It is. I'm glad you understand that." He put two fingers under my chin and lifted it so that our eyes were locked together. "I want you to know how much it's meant to me to have your support."

Guilt sliced through me as I thought about how often I'd wanted to rescind my support, to reverse the decision we'd made for him to strike out on his own. My gaze slid downward, and he released my chin.

"Lily?"

I looked up and met his stare.

"Lily, you mean everything to me, and your understanding is invaluable."

I couldn't stand it anymore. "Marcus, I . . . I haven't been as supportive as you seem to think."

His eyebrows creased. "What do you mean?"

"You know I've complained about wanting to move back to our house."

He smiled. "Yes. A few times."

I didn't know why he found that amusing, but I pushed on. "I may have only said it out loud a few times, but I've thought it a whole lot more than that."

"That's understandable."

"And when the renters set the kitchen on fire . . ." I frowned and shook my head. "I really resented that someone else had been allowed to do that to our house."

He laughed. "Yeah, I wasn't too happy about it either. But the kitchen looks great now."

"Yeah, after we had the damage repaired." I didn't want to think about that just now. "Anyway, my point is that I'm sorry I haven't been as supportive as I should have been." I paused. "But that's going to change. I know now that it doesn't matter where we live. The important thing is that we have each other."

"That's right," he said. "But it's also important that we actually spend time together, which is why I'm committing to you that I'm going to get home by dinner each night."

Doubtful that he could keep that commitment, I said, "As long as you try."

"No, Lily. I'm going to make it happen. That's one of the benefits of hiring the new engineer. We'll be able to spread the load now, and I'll be able to have a life."

"That sounds good." I just hoped it would actually come to pass.

# Chapter Thirty

After picking Natalie and Jackson up from John and Marcy, we headed home.

"Did you have fun with Grandma and Grandpa?" I asked as Marcus headed north on the freeway.

"Yes," Natalie said with a smile.

"Good." I glanced at Marcus. "I had fun with Daddy."

Marcus placed his hand on my knee and I set my hand on top of his, feeling closer to him than I had in a while.

It was November and the days were growing shorter. By the time we reached our town, the sun had set. I took a deep breath, gearing up to get back into the day-to-day routine. The children had fallen asleep, and I found myself dozing off, but when we stopped, I opened my eyes, ready to carry the children to bed.

"What are we doing here?" I asked Marcus as I stared at our house.

"Is there a problem?"

He smiled. "I'll just be a minute."

Confused and tired, I nodded. "Okay." I watched him walk to the front porch, although I couldn't see the door. I glanced at the children to make sure they hadn't woken, then waited for Marcus to return. A few moments later he did.

"Can you come inside?" he asked after opening my door.

"Why?"

His smile grew. "Please?"

"What about Natalie and Jackson?"

"Let's bring them in too."

I tilted my head to the side. "Marcus. I don't want to wake them up."

He laughed. "You don't want to leave them out here in the dark, do you?"

Exasperated, I said, "Can't we just go home? I'm really tired."

His lips twitched in a suppressed smile. "I'll get Natalie and you get Jackson." Then he went around to Natalie's door and began taking her out of her carseat.

Clearly, he wasn't going to change his mind. I sighed, then climbed out of the car and took Jackson out of his carseat. *What is going on? Why are we here?*

"All set?" Marcus asked me.

"Yeah." My tone showed my annoyance, but I followed him to the door anyway. He turned the knob and walked right in. Not sure what was going on, I walked in behind him.

"Surprise!"

Stunned to see Jeff and Trish, as well as Jordan and her husband Derek standing in the living room, I didn't understand what was going on. "What are you doing here?" I asked.

Their faces were wreathed in smiles.

"Welcome home, Lily," Marcus said.

That's when I noticed *our* furniture in the living room. Almost afraid to believe what I thought he was saying, I turned to him with a tentative smile. "Home? Here?"

He nodded, his eyes bright. "That's right. I wanted to surprise you."

Giddy with joy, I laughed. "You certainly did."

Greta rushed over to me, looking for attention. I squatted beside her, but then Jackson began fussing.

"Let's put the kids down," Marcus said. "Their rooms are ready for them."

Amazed that he'd pulled this off, I nodded. "Okay."

Once the children were tucked into their beds, we went back into the living room where Jordan had set up food for everyone to eat.

"I can't believe you guys did this," I said.

"It was all Marcus," Jeff said.

I looked at him, my eyes glowing with pleasure. "You're full of surprises, aren't you?"

He laughed. "I want to keep you on your toes."

We filled our plates, then sat at the table.

"So you were never looking for new renters after the Bartons moved out?" I asked.

Marcus laughed. "No. When they gave their notice, I knew it was time for us to move home."

I couldn't believe he'd kept it a secret from me for so long. I wanted to ask him if we could really afford to pay the mortgage, but didn't want to bring it up in front of everyone. Instead, I enjoyed everyone's company.

"Jordan," Marcus said, "thanks for overseeing everything."

"It wasn't too hard, not with all your stuff in storage." She glanced at me with a smile. "You'll have to organize your kitchen the way you want, but I unpacked most of the boxes."

Overwhelmed, tears filled my eyes. "You're amazing. Thank you so much."

"Seeing the look on your face was worth it," she said as she held Gabe on her lap.

"I'll miss having you at my house," Trish said. "I hope you and the children will come over often."

"We will." I laughed. "But once you get used to the peace and quiet you might not want us over too often."

"Oh no," she said. "It's going to be too quiet now."

<hr />

Once everyone had left, Marcus and I snuggled on the couch. It felt wonderful to be back in our home—the home we'd built together—but I still had some worries that needed to be put to rest.

"Marcus? How are we affording this?"

He ran a finger along my jawline, sending tingles through me. "Like I told you yesterday, my firm's doing pretty well now. Over the last little while I managed to put some money aside." He smiled. "We can afford to live in our house now. Money will be tight, but my income is steady enough now that we can do this." He leaned towards me and kissed me softly. "I know how important this is to you, so we'll make it work."

Thrilled that our life was settling back to normal, lightness filled my chest, and I nestled closer to him. "You're so good to me, Marcus. Thank you."

"I wanted to surprise you, so I didn't put the money in our shared account. I'll transfer it later." He chuckled. "I like having you in charge of our household expenses, but if money had started showing up in our account, I wouldn't have been able to pull this off without you knowing."

I laughed. "That's for sure."

"Are you ready to go to bed?" Marcus asked. Then added, "In our room?"

I let him pull me to my feet. "Absolutely."

Hand in hand, we walked down the hall, peeking in on Natalie and Jackson before going into our room. Greta raced past us and climbed onto her bed in the corner of our room, obviously knowing we were home again.

Laughing, I looked at Marcus, and when his gaze met mine, I knew without a doubt that home was wherever he and the children were.

"Thank you," I said as I stood in front of him.

"For what?" he said as a contented smile curved his mouth.

"For loving me, for doing so much for me." My voice softened. "For being the best husband I could have ever asked for."

"I love you, Lily," he said as his hand slid to the back of my neck.

"I love you too."

His lips descended toward mine, and when our mouths pressed together, love, peace, and joy mingled within me, and I knew that as imperfect as life could be, I had what I needed right in front of me and I knew that it was all worth it.

# Epilogue

One Year Later—Thanksgiving


I put the final touches on the salad, then turned to Marcus. "Are you done carving the turkey?"

"Yep. Just about."

"That looks delicious," Alyssa said as she looked over his shoulder. Then she rubbed her pregnant belly. "I just don't know how much I can fit in here."

Her baby was due in January, and I was excited to meet the little guy. "As long as you save room for the pumpkin pie."

She laughed. "Oh, I will."

I smiled, then after carrying the salad to the table, I walked to

Marcus's side. "Marcus?"

He turned to me with a smile. "What is it, sweetheart?"

Love and happiness swept over me as I gazed at my husband. "When you're done, can you tell everyone to come to the table?"

"Sure." He leaned towards me and kissed me, and a few moments later he went into the living room where his parents were talking to John and Marcy, who had come up from Las Vegas. After he spoke to them, they walked into the dining room.

"Where would you like us?" Trish asked me.

I smiled, happy she was there. Her cancer was in remission and her prognosis was good. "Wherever you'd like."

"Sit by me," Natalie said as she slid into an empty seat.

Nearly four, Natalie was thrilled to have both of her grandparents visiting, and had colored nearly an entire coloring book full of pictures to hand out.

Marcus picked up Jackson, who was nearly two, and placed him in a booster seat. "I'll sit by this little guy," he offered.

Appreciative of his constant willingness to help, I went into the kitchen to get the rest of the food. Alyssa and Ty carried the remaining side dishes into the dining room and set them on the table, and a moment later we began.

As I enjoyed the feast, I looked at the people sitting around my dining room table and was filled with an overwhelming feeling of gratitude. The relationships I enjoyed with these people—my family— were my most important possession. As happy as I was that we'd been back in our house for the last year, and that Marcus's business was thriving, the good people in my life beat all of that by a mile. After what we'd been through, I'd come to know that no matter what, nurturing those relationships—especially with my husband and children—was the most important and worthwhile thing for me to do.

Material possessions would come and go, but my family would always be there for me—and I would always be there for them. A smile of contentment curved my mouth.

I looked at Marcus and caught him looking at me, and when our eyes met, I knew our connection was solid and unbreakable. After the difficulties we'd faced, we'd only become closer, and now we looked to our future with confidence.

Challenges were inevitable, but we'd learned how to work together, and I knew that we would be able to face whatever life threw our way. We were a team, and we would stand together against whatever this imperfect life handed us.

Christine has always loved to read, but enjoys writing suspenseful novels as well. She has her own eReader and is not embarrassed to admit that she is a book hoarder. One of Christine's favorite activities is to go camping with her family and read, read, read while enjoying the beauty of nature.

Please visit Christine's website: christinekersey.com